Triolisme

An erotic short story collection by
Michelle Houston

www.unleashedink.com

TRIOLISME © 2015 by Michelle Houston

Individual Stories:

TRIOLISME

Published by Unleashed Ink

It goes without saying that in any writing endeavor, there are those that are behind the scenes that make writing possible. To all who have assisted me along the way - thank you.

And to my husband - who supports me even when my characters scare him a little bit - my heartfelt thanks and love. Without him, these stories would never have been written.

TRIOLISME

TABLE OF CONTENTS

Part 1:

When a man loves a woman …
and another man

Part 2:

When a woman loves a man …
and another woman

PART 1:

When a man loves a woman …

and another man

NINE BALL, CORNER POCKET

Grin on his face, Jesse leaned against the wall, his legs crossed at the ankle. A cue stood at attention in front of his groin, gripped between strong, folded arms. Across the pool table, Rhiannon leaned down and lined up her shot. The tip of her tongue licked between her lips as she concentrated.

"Two ball to the nine, corner pocket," she said.

Jesse spared the table a quick glance before giving a soft, derisive snort.

Glaring, Rhiannon's gaze lifted to his. "Don't think I can make it?"

"Not a chance, Honey" was his self-satisfied response.

"Oh really?" She pulled away from the table, striking her 'I can't believe you're doubting me' stance.

Jesse snorted again. He was accustomed to her moods and poses. When it came to pool, he was also familiar with her abilities, or rather, lack of them. After all, they'd played many similar games at his home, on the same table. They'd also played a different kind of sport, fucking each other senseless on its emerald green velvet. He could almost hear the tiny whimpers in her throat as she climaxed, her sweet juices running down her legs as he pounded into her from behind.

"Care to make a wager on that?" She snapped, interrupting his sordid thoughts.

Jesse startled, realizing he hadn't heard what she'd said. He asked her to repeat herself. When she did, he grinned. "Rhiannon, I'm not going to take your money."

"I wasn't talking about money darlin'. I meant something more wicked." As she spoke, her eyes danced with mischief.

Intrigued, he pushed off from the wall and stepped towards the pool table, leaning on its edge, "How wicked?"

"Mmmm," she purred, licking her lips. "How about if I miss this shot, you get to fuck my tight little ass?"

Straining to think straight at her announcement, Jesse wondered what the catch was. "And if you make the shot?" was his faintly suspicious reply.

Quick as a whip, she retorted, "I get to watch you get your tight little ass fucked." Her amusement was rapidly increasing.

Bingo, there was the catch, although somehow, it didn't seem such a bad trade. Rhiannon had been hinting about wanting to watch him and another man for a while, ever since he'd confessed his interest in gay porn. Her idea contained a certain dark appeal.

Before he lost his nerve, he agreed to her sinful dare. "You're on babe, but on one condition, if you win I still get to fuck your tight little ass sometime soon, just the way you've always wanted. You can't fool me, I know you're dying for it."

He was tempted to startle her with a sudden noise, but the glare Rhiannon shot stopped him. Sometimes it sucked to be with someone so long that they knew you well enough to predict your next move. But on reflection, given the killer blowjob Rhiannon had given him the night before, it was a welcome trade off, having that person know your personal hot spots.

The tip of her tongue flicked out again, causing him to squirm as his attention was drawn to her lips. The way she stroked the pool stick didn't help his peace of mind, either.

Drawing the cue back, she slid it slowly forward again, almost tapping the cue ball. Jesse's attention was further divided as she widened her stance, took a deep breath, and slowly swung her arm back.

The cue slid forward between her fingers and Jesse held his breath. Regardless of the outcome, they both knew Rhiannon's ass would no longer be virgin territory, but he wasn't so certain about his. As much as he worried, he found himself hoping she made the shot.

The two ball gently tapped the nine and for a moment, it hugged the rim, before falling into the pocket. In that moment, Jesse knew Rhiannon had triumphed. He only hoped that in the end, he'd win as well.

* * *

After her victory, Rhiannon planted a quick kiss on Jesse's lips and then headed home for the night, leaving him to dwell on what was to come.

9

Jesse brooded over his situation as he sat in front of the TV, intently watching several rented videos showing gay men in various erotic situations. For two days, he rushed home from work, first checking his answering machine, before playing a video and lubricating his hands.

He masturbated to scenes of construction workers, college roommates and military men, but his favorite movie featured two men in a pool hall. He stroked his cock raw as he repeatedly watched one man bugger the other with the butt end of a pool cue, before the cue wielder fucked his willing victim.

It gave Jesse an added thrill when he pressed a finger inside his ass, wriggling it as he jerked himself off. He'd even been tempted to try something a bit firmer and bigger, like the mini-vibrator Rhiannon kept in the nightstand, but he hadn't been able to work up the nerve.

As evening fell on the third day, Jesse's cell phone rang and he glanced at the display. Rhiannon had finally decided to call. As he answered, loud techno-music assaulted his ears. He could barely hear Rhiannon's shouts, but eventually he made out what she was saying.

"I'll be at your place in about an hour. Wear those jeans of yours I like, and nothing else, and darlin' - make sure you have the lube and a few condoms handy."

A click sounded in his ear as the loud music, and Rhiannon's voice, was replaced by a dial tone. His hand suddenly shaking, Jesse ended the call and then rushed to pick up the clutter in his apartment before company arrived.

An hour later, he'd just finished clearing the mess when the doorbell rang.

Closing the dishwasher and flicking the switch, he surveyed the apartment as he headed to the front door. The rented videos were hidden, the couch cushions were flipped over and he'd moved the lube into the bedroom. The tube now sat on the dresser, next to a full box of condoms. Everything looked normal, except he was wearing jeans that were slightly baggy over his hips, no boxers, no shirt - and he was about to have sex with a man he'd never met.

Forcing a smile to his lips, he concentrated on steadying his hand; first one deep breath, then another. Closing his eyes, he pictured Rhiannon leaning over the pool table, her legs spread

10

and her asshole lubed and ready. Glancing at his hand again, he noticed it was steady, but he also caught sight of the increasing bulge in his jeans. With a nervous flourish, Jesse opened the door to the wonders that were to come.

Jesse's eyes widened as they trailed over Rhiannon's 'friend.' It only took a moment for him to realize he knew Neil, though normally, Rhiannon's editor was dressed in a nice suit and sported slicked back hair. He oozed heterosexual vibes and turned many a feminine head.

Yet, the man standing in front of him was rugged, dressed in tight black cargos and a black button-up shirt with the sleeves rolled up. His tattoos were clearly visible and a very noticeable hard-on strained against the seam of his pants.

"Jesse, I hear I get to pop your cherry," Neil taunted. He placed a hand against Jesse's chest and gently pushed him back into the apartment. Slowly sliding his hand down his willing victim's torso, to the waist of his jeans, he hooked his finger in a belt loop and pulled the unresisting man towards him.

Rhiannon closed the door behind them.

"Between you and me, I think I'm going to love every minute of it. I have a feeling you will as well." Neil's words contained an almost addictive seductiveness.

Jesse gulped silently and opened his mouth to respond, but he never got a chance. Neil leaned forward and pressed his lips to Jesse's, sparking sudden feral desire. Almost instantly, Jesse's cock grew stiffer. Unfulfilled fantasies began to roar through his mind. The texture of those male lips was similar to Rhiannon's, but different somehow. They were firmer and more impatient.

Neil took possession of Jesse's mouth, thrusting his tongue past willingly parted lips. The insistent organ searched out its wet and warm opposite number. Neil's hands slid around Jesse's hips, pulling the shell-shocked man against him.

Jesse admired this display of dominance, even as he submitted. Groin to groin now, Jesse ground his hips slowly, igniting a trail of need in them both.

It turned him on more knowing that Rhiannon was watching he and her best friend dueled for control.

Jesse saw Neil pull back to look at him, and he knew what Neil would see because Rhiannon had told him often enough. Neil would notice the way his hair spiked slightly; he'd notice a

11

crescent of thick lashes lying against tanned cheeks. Jesse understood his own qualities, the perfect working class construction worker, toned, tanned, and sexy as hell. Judging by the equally wild and intoxicating looks of his partner, it was, he guessed, going to be a wild ride for them all.

As Jesse's eyes locked on Neil's, his seducer leaned down and kissed him again. At that moment, Jesse noticed the light floral scent of Rhiannon's perfume. She'd moved to stand beside him. He felt her carefully grasp his hand.

Half directing, half-pulling, Rhiannon led the two men to the bedroom. Jesse allowed himself to be guided backward; to let Rhiannon and Neil set the pace. It was nice to have the decision and details taken out of his hands.

As the door closed with a soft click, Jesse pulled away from Neil. For a second, the sensual haze cleared from his mind and the true reality of his situation dawned. Panic began to creep in.

"I can't do this," he whispered, his eyes darting to Rhiannon in a mute plea.

"Shhh baby," she whispered, stepping between the two men. Raising her hands to Jesse's chest, she also nodded slightly towards Neil, before turning back to reassure her boyfriend, "Nothing's going to happen that you don't want."

Slowly twining her fingers in the soft golden curls covering her lover's chest, she coaxed his lips down to hers. They kissed passionately, as her hands roamed over his ribs, down to the well-worn buttons of his Levis. Undoing them, she slipped his jeans over his ass and gravity took its effect.

Jesse watched as she kneeled down in front of him and lifted his feet one after the other, until he'd stepped out of the worn, blue denims. "Just relax baby, and let me take care of you." She straightened up and met his gaze.

With a quick flick of her tongue to dampen her lips, she leaned forward slightly and kissed the head of his cock. A small drop of pre-cum oozed to the tip and she teased him, swirling her tongue over the glistening drop, before sucking him into her mouth. She tasted an inch, then pulled back, each delay driving him wild. Another inch, then again she backed off.

Slowly, sensually, she aroused him to fever pitch. His hands twisted in her perfectly made up hair, pulling the pins free and leaving her long tresses dangling down her back. Soon, he forgot all about the other man in the room, watching his beautiful siren have her way with his willing flesh.

Her hands tenderly cupped his ball sac, playing gently with the sensitive skin. Moaning softly, he arched into her mouth, thrusting his cock in a steady rhythm. Muted sucking sounds filled the room, his groans a low accompaniment.

As Rhiannon pulled back, he could hear the sound of her mouth on his flesh and his eyes flickered open. He saw Neil standing to his left, naked. Only the occasional tattoo covered his tanned flesh. Then Neil's ink black eyes met his and Jesse couldn't look away, even when Rhiannon's satiny mouth moved back over his straining erection.

He watched, fascinated, as Neil cupped his own cock and he gently stroked himself. Desperately, Jesse wanted to feel it pound into him and stretch him to his limits. His fears were soon pushed to the back of his mind when Rhiannon's mouth drove him back to the brink, before she suddenly pulled away again.

Now, he watched as her lovely lips closed around Neil's cock, sucking it deep within her warm, velvety mouth. Jealousy pulsed inside him as he gazed, but not because his woman had her lips wrapped around another man's cock. He wanted to taste Neil's flesh against his tongue as well.

Dropping to his knees, he gently pushed Rhiannon away and moved to take her place. Hesitantly, he kissed Neil's stiffness, tasting the salty essence leaking from the bulging tip. Taking a deep breath, he opened his lips and sucked the inviting phallus deep into his mouth. For a moment, he gagged, then backed off, remembering past girlfriends and their tentative attempts. Trying again, he took Neil's erection more deeply into his mouth and then pulled back.

Softly, Neil's hands came to rest on Jesse's head, guiding him without pressure until he found a comfortable rhythm.

Jesse's eyes now focused completely on Neil, watching for subtle clues. He wasn't sure what to do next. When Neil's lids fluttered closed, and his Adam's apple bobbed, Jesse knew he was doing okay. Filled with confidence, he sucked harder, stroking his hands up and down Neil's thighs, enjoying the feel of the wiry hair beneath his palms.

Jesse knew Neil was close to orgasm when he felt the man's hands tighten in his hair. He knew because, when Rhiannon went down on him, he reacted the same way, holding her face still as he fucked her throat.

Jesse watched as Neil's eyes opened suddenly and his nostrils flared a little. Then, out of the corner of his eye, he saw what had drawn Neil's attention away. Rhiannon was slowly undressing, her hands running over her stomach and thighs, caressing her smooth skin. For a moment, his hands itched to return to his sweet love's softness, but as drops of pre-cum leaked from Neil's slit, he returned his attention to his male paramour.

Only her heels, hose, and garter remained as Rhiannon knelt, once again, next to Jesse. Carefully lying on her stomach, she shifted as close to him as possible and then softly parted his ass cheeks, sliding her tongue along the cleft. Jesse trembled as she rimmed him, her tongue slipping past his ass-ring. Many times before he had tasted of her forbidden crevice, sampling the tangy, sweaty flesh, imagining it being done to him, but he had never been able to ask for it.

Jesse could feel Neil's gaze on him, as he experienced this delight for the first time.

Jesse felt Rhiannon pull her tongue from his ass, giving the crevice one last deep lick before moving away. Sucking Neil's cock deep, he focused his attention solely on the taste and sensation of the velvety flesh in his mouth. A whisper of sound behind him barely gave him warning before Rhiannon pressed a finger against his sphincter and pushed.

He jerked in response. Instantly Neil was soothing him – tenderly brushing his hands over his face and shoulder. He quickly guided Jesse back into a steady rhythm, as Rhiannon's finger slipped deeper, and was joined by another, provoking a curious tingling.

Minutes passed as the three reveled in their exploration. Then Rhiannon pulled away from Jesse and stood. Stepping around the two men, she moved towards the bedside table and grabbed the tube of lubricant, squeezing some into her palm.

She rubbed her hands together, before carefully spreading it between her buttocks. She forced a finger inside her anus and wiggled her hand. Jesse's eyes almost crossed. He swallowed a hint of panic, as Neil pulled his cock free from Jesse's ass and moved to stand behind her.

She slipped her finger free and held her ass cheeks apart as Neil thrust his lube-coated digits deep into her ass. With his other hand, he guided her onto her belly across the bed, her feet planted firmly on the floor.

Jesse watched as Neil forced his fingers in and out of her butt, gently twisting them as he did. He was intrigued by the look on his lover's face, as her ass fought against the invasion. Small streams of fire flooded his body, his cock hard and throbbing as he imagined it was his fingers up Rhiannon's ass, while Neil manipulated his virgin sphincter.

"Spread your legs further," Neil demanded, as he settled his body between her silky thighs. His palm firmly planted against her back, he pinned her legs against the bed with his, and continued to fuck her with his fingers. The fire that raced through Jesse soon turned into an inferno, as Rhiannon responded to the sensual invasion, arching her hips, guiding Neil deeper.

She lifted her body from the bed, and moved her hand down to her clit. Jesse moved closer, his emotions whirling as his hands stroked his cock of their own volition.

Fisting his cock, Jesse watched as Rhiannon bucked against Neil, timing her finger's thrusts to his until, together, they fucked her into a quivering orgasm.

It was a breathtaking sight. In that moment, looking at the satisfied look on his girlfriend's face, he knew she'd made the right choice for him. Neil was patient, tender, and obviously skilled.

In a moment of brazenness, Jesse knelt on the bed next to Rhiannon, reached back, and parted his own ass-cheeks. His gaze locked on Rhiannon's, nervous as hell, he attempted a smile. He wasn't certain how successful he was.

Jesse couldn't quite believe he'd parted his own ass cheeks, but as Neil moved behind him and slid the tip of the lubricant tube into his ass, he no longer cared. His body demanded satisfaction, even as his mind rebelled. He knew there would be discomfort and maybe even pain.

Watching Rhiannon's face had underlined that fact. He knew her well; enough to know she'd tried to hide it. He also knew he had nerves in that sensitive area that a woman didn't. If Rhiannon had adjusted, and even enjoyed it, he could only imagine what he would feel.

And he was tired of waiting, wondering what it would be like; of living with the constant craving.

Taking a deep breath, he tried to prepare for the sensation of a handful of cool gel in and around his ass. When he experienced it, he trembled as he anticipated what was to follow.

He sensed Neil shift away, and he turned his head when he heard foil rustling. He saw Neil standing next to Rhiannon; she was sliding a condom over his weeping cock. Other than the sweet spread of Rhiannon's pussy lips, he wondered if he'd ever seen a more erotic sight. Her dainty hands slid over the latex coated flesh, spreading a layer of lube over Neil's eager erection. Her eyes met Jesse's, and she smiled her gentle siren's smile.

Unable to stand the suspense, his fingers clenched the sheets and he closed his eyes. The feel of gentle hands on his ass made him tremble. Neil moved to stand against him, reminiscent of the way he'd pinned Rhiannon down. A palm pressed against his back and Jesse took a deep breath.

"Relax." Neil's cultured tones contrasted sharply with the motifs that decorated his body. For a moment, Jesse wondered what had motivated Neil. He'd been tattooed at least six different times.

Relaxing, as a fingernail tapped against his anus, Jesse took a deep breath. Then, a long finger slipped past his ring. Soon, it was joined by a second. Slowly, they worked in and out of his ass, pushing against the ring of nerves. Twitching slightly, Jesse arched back into the touch.

It was like nothing he'd ever felt before. He had always been tempted to include ass play in his sex life, but before Rhiannon, no other woman had been interested. Rhiannon was willing to fuck his ass with a strap on, but first, she wanted him to be fully breached by a man. With that lucky pool shot, she'd made her requirement a reality, and fulfilled a fantasy for them both.

Lost in the sensations, with sparks of pleasure racing throughout his body, he didn't at first notice the pressure had eased. The first touch of Neil's cock against his ass ring quickly brought his attention back to the present. Trying to relax was hard.

"Wait a moment, Neil." Rhiannon soft voice stilled the pressure against Jesse's ass. Opening his eyes, Jesse watched Rhiannon settle in front of him. She knelt, with her legs parted. Reaching down, she separated her slick pussy lips.

Dipping her fingers deeply, she coated them in her juices and spread the smooth essence of her arousal on Jesse's lips. Licking the sweetness, he closed his eyes and savored the moment.

Distracted, he didn't notice Neil pressing against his ring, until Neil's glans had slipped inside him. A moment passed, and he felt a curious stretching sensation as Neil's cock completely penetrated his ass. Gritting his teeth, he waited for the pain, but there wasn't much. As Neil moved within him, Jesse's fists gripped the sheets and he followed his lover's rhythm. Within moments, they were working together in a steady thrust, then withdrawal.

His ass full of cock for the first time, Jesse watched as Rhiannon thrust two fingers deep into her pussy, her other hand playing with her clit. Both hands soon grew wet with her juices, as she fucked herself into another orgasm. The scent of her arousal flooded his senses.

Clenching at each of Neil's thrusts, Jesse arched back into each thrust. His cock steadily leaked pre-cum and his balls tightened. Jesse knew it was all about to end; he was about to orgasm with a man's cock sawing in and out of his ass. With each thrust, his erection bobbed. With each withdrawal, his ass begged for more.

Thrust and withdrawal; grind and clench. Over and over, the two lovers worked against, then with each other, drawing both of them closer to the inevitable.

Animalistic grunts echoed off the walls, and Jesse was nearly too far-gone to notice the sounds were coming from his own mouth.

His ass begged for each hard thrust and his cock pulsed with need. Balls tight, he ground his hips against the sheets as Neil pushed deep inside him. Clenching his lover tight, he locked his legs and jerked against the sheets. Weird sensations racked his body as he climaxed. Hot, sticky squirts shot from his throbbing flesh, creating a warm, tacky pool on the bed. Convulsing with each spurt of his orgasm, he clenched tighter, pulling Neil into the vortex.

Closing his eyes, Jesse arched against Neil as his new lover pounded into him. Within moments, Neil's slight weight collapsed onto Jesse's back. Vaguely, Jesse heard Rhiannon gasp as she climaxed a third time, but he was too far-gone to care. All that mattered was the steadily softening cock in his ass, the weight of a man lying on him, and the cum leaking from his own cock.

Heaving a soft sigh, he shifted, forcing Neil to roll off. With sleepy eyes, he watched as Neil pulled the latex from his cock, and tossed it in the trash. Jesse slid towards Rhiannon, making room for Neil on the bed. Pressing his face against Rhiannon's moist flesh, Jesse took a deep breath, as he struggled to bring sanity to a world made up entirely of tingling nerves.

"Mmmmm," he managed, as Rhiannon nuzzled her pussy against his lips.

Tentatively, he stuck his tongue out and wiggled it, as she ground against him. Her fingers occasionally brushed against his forehead. As he gradually collected his thoughts, his limbs still deliciously lethargic, Jesse rolled over just enough for Rhiannon to mount his face and grind herself to another screaming orgasm.

The bed dipped as Neil settled beside him, and Jesse shifted in response, spooning with his new lover. Within moments, Rhiannon had joined them, snuggling her back against Jesse's chest.

Lying there, the three held each other as they adjusted to the changes one night had caused. Jesse wasn't certain how Neil was going to fit into their relationship, but the fact Rhiannon had chosen him, instead of any number of bi and gay men she knew, spoke volumes. He knew Rhiannon had been attracted to her editor since day one, and that despite their attraction, they had become good friends.

Jesse felt Neil smile against his neck, but he wasn't quite sure why.

"You know she set you up right?"

Neil's voice startled Jesse for a moment as he floated in a haze of contentment. Shifting himself and Rhiannon so that he could see both their faces, Jesse asked, "What do you mean?"

"I've been working with her for the last six weeks, teaching her to play pool. She used to suck, but lately, she's gotten rather good."

Jesse met Rhiannon's guilty gaze. He wanted to be upset that she had manipulated things, but he knew that would be unfair. She had given him something that they both wanted, but that he wouldn't have been able to ask for. With that winning shot, she had freed him to enjoy his sexuality.

Leaning down, he pressed his lips to hers, hoping she could tell all the things he wanted to say, but couldn't.

Behind him, Neil shifter until his lips touched the lobe of Jesse's left ear. "And over the last six weeks, we've made a lot of plans, for both of your tight asses. Tomorrow, all three of us are going to play nine ball, and winner fucks both losers."

Michelle Houston

THEIR HAREM GIRL

*The Naughty Woman's Guide To
Spicing Up Your Sex Life*

*1. Food is fun to play with
2. Think "bondage of love"
3. You need a spanking, you naughty
girl!
4. Sensual Massage & candlelight are
not antique concepts
5. Play with some battery operated toys
6. Role play & dress up—much more
fun than when we were kids*

Andrea paused as she reached number 6. Now there was an idea she hadn't considered in a long time. Skimming down to the end of the article, she found the author's suggestions for roles to act out.

*Be an Indian maiden to his cavalry soldier,
a mistress to his slave, a captive to his pirate,
a school girl to his principal. Be anything that
your imagination can create a scenario for.
This isn't a movie, so it doesn't have to be
fancy. Focus on the fantasy itself instead.*

Her mind already running wild with the scenario she wanted to act out, Andrea grabbed her purse and keys, and headed out the door. She had less than three hours before her husband and their roommate came home from work and a whole lot of errands to run.

A little over two hours later she pulled into the driveway and popped the trunk. Grabbing the bags from the costume store, the grocery store and the adult shop near the interstate, she hurried inside to set the stage. She was about to act out her secret fantasy. Butterflies ran rampant in her stomach at the very idea.

After a quick shower, she donned her outfit and set about turning the master bedroom into a fantasy setting, perfect for the three of them to play in. She carefully draped her silk shirts over the bedside lamps, casting a softer glow about the room. Silk throw pillows replaced the normal bed pillows. The bed sheet and blanket were tossed in the closet, leaving only the bottom sheet. She had just finished setting the tray of fruits and wine on the nightstand when she heard her husband's car in the driveway. Grabbing her last prop, she hurried down the hall to the entry way and dropped to her knees just as the door opened.

"Honey we're ... what the hell?" Ryan's husky voice sent a shudder of sensual awareness through her. Ever since he had started dating her husband and then moved in with them, Ryan had been a part of the lives, sexual and not. He had become her best friend, her greatest ally, and the second love of her life.

Holding out the printed paper she had rolled up and tied with a ribbon, she winked slowly at Ryan. With a grin he stepped aside for Daniel.

"Someone's feeling playful," Ryan said, reaching down for the scroll. Holding it out to her husband, he winked back at her.

Andrea could feel Daniel's eyes trailing over her for a moment before he pulled the paper from the ribbon and started reading aloud.

> *Please accept this slave as an offer of friendship between our two nations.*
> *She has been well trained in the fine arts of pleasing a man and it is my fondest hope that she brings you pleasure.*

His voice soft and teasing, Ryan responded "Ah, a new concubine to add to my harem." Andrea allowed herself a slight smile as Ryan continued to play along. "Let's see how well-trained she truly is."

With an arrogant wave of his hand he motioned for her to follow him and walked into the bedroom. Gracefully gaining her feet, Andrea waited until Daniel moved past her and followed. The silk of her belly dancer costume skirt rustled slightly as she walked slowly, giving the men time to get settled. The tiny bells on the anklet she wore jingled with each step.

As she walked into the room, she found Ryan already on the bed, reclining against the pillows. Daniel joined him, leaning back against his chest. The tray of food had been moved to the bed, and while she stood there, awaiting their instructions, she watched as Daniel slowly fed their lover a strawberry.

"Dance for us."

Andrea bit back a smile. The only thing Ryan liked more than watching her dance was watching her go down on her husband. She was glad she had taken the time to factor his predictability in. Crossing the room to the stereo, she pushed play on the CD she had just bought. She wasn't certain just what instruments were being played, but it was the kind of music she could imagine played during a movie set in a harem. Slow, deep and foreign, the music had a seductive quality all is own.

She lifted her hands over her head and slowly rotated her wrists, then softly thrust her hips. The bells attached to her costume's belt jingled. Her nipples tightened against her silk top, straining against the thin material. Sleeveless and ending at her midriff, it covered her about as well as a bikini top, leaving most of her stomach exposed. Her skirt rode low on her hips. With the predatory way that Ryan watched her movements, she felt like a harem girl, dancing for her master. Her only goal was to please him.

As she continued to dance, Ryan's hands absently started caressing Daniel's chest, unbuttoning his shirt and pulling it free of his slacks. Her husband's smooth chest was slowly bared to her view. Although he wasn't most women's idea of drop-dead gorgeous, especially given his fair-skinned complexion, the sight of his wiry frame always set her mouth watering. Add in his dark eyes and short cropped dark hair, and toss him in a suit, and he was her idea of a wet dream. There was just something about knowing what his hands and mouth could do that made up for any lack of muscle mass. The other women who had passed him by didn't know what they were missing, but that was okay by her.

In high school she had always been more attracted to the nerdy guys in the science and math clubs than the jocks, which was why her strong attraction for Ryan surprised her at first. He was the definition of gorgeous, with rich chocolate eyes, a deep sun-kissed skin tone, hair a shade too long to be fashionable, and hands big enough to hold both a woman's wrists in one while he slowly fucked her senseless. Yet he had a sharp mind behind his brown eyes that tended to surprise everyone.

Quick to laugh, he was even quicker to passion. Which is what had first drawn Daniel to him, that quicksilver flash of lust as they had shaken hands at works.

Losing herself in the fantasy, Andrea slowly turned around, rotating her waist to show off her ass. She jerked her hips, setting the tiny bells on her body jingling. Across the room Daniel groaned. Looking over her shoulder, she saw that Ryan had unzipped Daniel's pants and slowly stroked his cock.

"Come here slave." Ryan's voice betrayed his growing arousal.

Andrea stopped dancing and glided across the room. Climbing onto the bed, she knelt beside Ryan's hip.

"Take my other slave into your mouth."

After licking her lips, she leaned down and wrapped them around Daniel's cock head. He moaned softly as he thrust up against her, his fingers sliding through her hair. Her lips pressed tight around him, Andrea sucked his length into her mouth, relaxing her throat to take all of him.

"Mmm, that's good. You have been trained well."

The salty taste of her husband's pre-cum teased her taste buds. Sucking harder, she worked his cock slowly in and out of her mouth. Her pussy damp against her costume, she tightened her thighs trying to glide the damp material against her pussy. She could feel her husband's cock pulsing in her mouth as his orgasm approached. She wiggled her hips, trying to generate friction on her clit.

A sharp slap against her ass stopped her movements. She jerked back in shock, her gaze meeting Ryan's. A twinkle lit his brown eyes, lending him a boyish air.

"Enough of that. You move when I tell you to move and not before." His movements deft, he unzipped his own pants and freed his cock. "Now let's see how good a cock-sucker you really are."

Daniel moved to the side as she leaned down to take Ryan's cock into her mouth. Although shorter than her husband, he was wider, making him a bit of a mouthful, but she loved his girth. It complemented Daniel's length perfectly.

Teasing him, she nipped lightly at his head before sliding down, engulfing him in the velvet heat of her mouth. He pulsed against her tongue, throbbing with each beat of his heart. His hands fisted in her hair, almost ruthlessly guiding her up and down on his cock, just the way he liked it. The bells around her waist jingled with each jerk of her body as Andrea allowed her lover to guide her motions.

"Oh yes, you have been well trained. I'll have to send along my thanks to your former master." Ryan's hands moved down her shoulders, pushing her away before he moved away from her. "But for now, I wish to discover what other training you have had."

With an impervious flick of his wrist, he motioned Daniel to lie on his back. His movements graceful, Ryan climbed off of the bed and moved to stand behind her.

His hands firm, he started removing her outfit. As he unzipped the top, he tossed it aside and his hands cupped her breasts, rolling the nipples between his fingers. "Take off your skirt."

Her hands shaky with desire, Andrea slowly lifted her hips from her heels and pulled the material down to her knees. Angling to her side, she pulled first one leg free then the other. All that remained was the belt around her waist and her matching anklet. As she leaned forward, she wiggled her ass, drawing Ryan's gaze to the plug she had inserted into her ass-bud.

"Perfect," he drawled, his voice deep and husky. Andrea trembled in response as his hands glided over her ass, caressing her. "Mount my slave."

Daniel's eyes widened as she slowly crawled over him. Fully dressed, he lay passively beneath her as she gripped his cock and slowly thrust down, driving him into her pussy. His hips jerked as she squeezed tight, her body begging for more. Ryan's hands continued to caress her body as she slowly rode Daniel, her hips rocking back and forth, grinding against his pelvis.

Ryan's deft movements pulled the plug from her ass, and even before she had time to mourn the loss, he was kneeling behind her and thrusting hard past her tight ring.

"Oh god!' she gasped, her anus on fire as he pushed his cock into her. Although she had enjoyed Daniel's cock there, it wasn't something Ryan had ever tried to do to her. Now as his girth stretched her she tried to jerk away, but Daniel's body held her pinned. There was nowhere she could go.

His hands gently against her hips, he pulled her back tighter against him, seating his cock into her ass to the balls. Daniel thrust up against her, and Andrea whimpered at the intense sensation of two cocks within her.

The bells around her waist jingled with each thrust as Ryan slowly began to fuck her, his larger frame dwarfing her as he pushed down against her husband, positioning her for his deep thrusts. It was everything she had fantasized about from the moment the article sparked her interest. Being taken by both her men, fucked and filled by them both at the same time. She was their slave, helpless to do anything but enjoy their claiming. Her pussy ached, as she clenched tight. Behind her Ryan groaned. "Do it again."

Already out of breath, Andrea squeezed her pussy and ass tight, milking the cocks within her.

Ryan's hands tightened on her hips, as he started pounding against her. Beneath her, Daniel's thrusts fell into rhythm. Rather than one thrusting as the other withdrew, they both thrust together. It was enough to make her scream. The tray of fruits hit the floor as the hardboard slammed against the wall under the force of their movements.

Beneath her, Daniel thrashed slightly, his wiry frame tight against hers. With a soft grunt his orgasm washed over him, his cum a warm rush in her pussy. Behind her Ryan doubled his efforts, his cock thrusting hard within her ass. Moving a hand from her waist, he started playing with her clit, pinching the little nub between his fingers as she jerked against him. Soft moans escaped her lips as she ground down against Daniels' softening cock. His eyes flickered open and met hers, and with a soft grin, he cupped her breasts and pinched her nipples roughly.

Yelping, she shuddered as Ryan's fingers tightened on her clit until a tidal wave of pleasure-pain rushed over her, radiating out from her pussy and nipples. With a soft scream she came, collapsing against her husband. Behind her, Ryan pulled out of her ass and she felt warm spurts of cum landing against her back.

His hands firm, he rubbed his cum into her skin, while she lay there trying to regain her breath. Sliding to the side, she curled against Daniel as Ryan shifted on the bed, moving to lie spooned against her back.

"Where on earth did you get the idea for this babydoll?" Ryan asked, his hands caressing little circles on her thigh.

"Um, I was reading an article in a magazine about spicing up your sex life through things like role playing and dress-up and I remembered all those romances I read during my late teens. My favorites were the ones set in harems, where a captive woman is turned into a pleasure slave by a domineering master. They never got into too much detail, but they were enough to get me hot then."

"Mmm," Ryan breathed against her neck, "I definitely wouldn't mind acting this one out again in greater detail."

Daniel's chest rumbled under her cheek as he chuckled. "Neither would I. But next time, you get to be the other slave. She almost sucked me off, then you made her quit."

WANDERING WHERE LED

Kara gave a quick jerk to the reins, drawing *Wandering Scotsman* to a stop as her host walked toward her, arms wide. "Kara, *bella*!" He kissed her cheeks and stepped back, holding her hands in his. "I'm so delighted you decided to grace us with your presence, and with your prized stallion."

Behind her, the stallion in question snorted and tossed his head, shaking his dark mane at the attention. Smothering her smirk at his antics, she gave another tug to his reins to show her disapproval. Ian, or the *Wandering Scotsman* as he was called when in full regalia, neighed softly in response, acknowledging the silent chastening.

"So, where is the mare you wanted my Scotsman to cover?" Kara asked.

Her fellow pony owner dropped her hands and motioned to one of the stable attendants waiting behind him. The naked woman's leather heels tapped on the hardwood floor as she moved deeper into Aaron's playground. Hardcore into pony play, he had built the special stable on his property and routinely had anywhere from 20 to 40 Dominants and subs running around, acting out their own fantasies. The curious, those who were tempted but uncertain, were able to play the role of attendants, performing menial, and often sexual, tasks requested of them.

Kara often wondered if some of the ponies actually slept in their stalls, as some had lavish beds and others simply contained padded tables and benches.

"Actually, *Mon Chere*, it's *Daddy's Toy* I want him to mount." The attendant returned, leading a young male, his blond hair carefully braided and tied back, revealing striking features. "He's been fighting the bit, not adjusting as quickly as I would prefer. I want him to truly get the full experience."

Kara's breath caught at the idea. She had allowed Ian to mount and, thanks to a strap-on, be mounted by several other submissives--all mares. As far as she knew, he had never been with another man, but the idea intrigued her. From the silence behind her, she knew he was considering the idea as well.

He would have whinnied or shifted away if the idea repulsed him. As her gaze trailed over the approaching stallion, she could see the appeal. *Daddy's Toy* barely stood as tall as his attendant, who couldn't be more than five-eight. With his delicate features and long blond hair, he could pass for her brother; her attractive, well-hung younger brother. He looked to be about ten years younger than her own 35, placing him about five years younger than Ian.

When the stallion reached them, Aaron took the lead from the attendant and dismissed her back to her corner. "So Bella, what do you think?"

Kara shrugged, trying to be nonchalant when inside she was trembling with excitement. "If *Daddy's Toy* accepts him, then I have no problem with the arrangement." They both looked at the blonde stallion. His nostrils were flared, and his blue eyes sparkled with excitement as they traced over Ian's muscular frame.

She knew what he saw had to be tempting. Ian's long dark reddish brown hair, creamy skin, and athletic body turned many heads wherever they went.

Aaron lead his stallion to the stall, and Kara followed at a slower pace, leading her *Wandering Scotsman*, giving him time to prepare himself mentally. As they watched, Aaron guided *Daddy's Toy* right up to a small padded table that stood chest high on him. Another attendant stepped into the room, his cock hard and colored a dusky red thanks to a cock-ring. As Kara led her Scotsman further into the room, the attendant drew a step-stool out of a cabinet and placed it at the base of the table, then grasped *Daddy's Toy*'s lead.

With a click of his tongue, he coaxed the stallion onto the stool and leaned him over the padded table. Behind Kara, Ian started shifting from foot to foot. Reaching back, she grasped his cock and found it hard, his balls tight against his body. Her pussy clenched at the knowledge that he was as turned on by the idea of his covering another male as she was of allowing it to happen.

When the attendant finished lubricating the blonde pony's anus, he turned to Kara. "Mistress, do you wish me to ring his cock?"

After giving her Scotsman's cock a squeeze, she nodded. The man dropped to his knees before Ian and pulled his cock into his mouth. After giving a few quick sucks, he pulled back and slipped the ring up Ian's cock. Almost immediately, his cock swelled, the veins popping out, the flesh turning a dark, angry red.

Reaching up, she unbuckled Ian's harness and pulled the bit from his mouth. She raised up on her toes and pressed a kiss against his lips, thrusting her tongue into his mouth. Moving closer, she pressed her chest against him, even as she was aware of the attendant still kneeling at his feet, the back of his bald head trapped between their groins.

As she pulled back, she saw a familiar glazed look in Ian's eyes. Patting his cheek, she let him go. "Enjoy yourself," she whispered. Ian smiled and moved to stand behind the other stallion. Slowly, he ran his hands over the blond's legs and back, stroking softly and soothingly, until *Daddy's Toy* moaned in response.

Aaron moved to stand by his stallion's head and cupped his chin in his hands.

When the attendant at her feet moved to stand, Kara lightly placed a hand over his shoulder and held him in place. If he really wanted to, he could have stood, but he sank back down. Idly, she stroked her fingertips over his shoulder as she watched her lover make his move.

Unlike Ian's tail, which was attached to a butt plug firmly planted in his anus, *Daddy's Toy*'s tail was attached to a slender belt that encircled his hips. Ian shifted the blond's tail out of his way and grasping his cock in his hand, pressed it against the Toy's greased anus, and thrust forward. Kara watched, breath held, as his cock disappeared inch by inch.

Her eyes widened as Aaron unzipped his pants and pulled out his cock. *Daddy's Toy* eagerly accepted it, slurping on it loudly as Ian started thrusting into his ass. Groans from all three men filled the room, sending a shiver through her body. Still stroking the attendant's shoulder, she pulled her skirt up, baring her pussy. The bald attendant buried his face against her pussy, his tongue stroking the seam of her pussy lips.

Kara dug her fingernails into the back of his head, grinding her pussy against his face. Her gaze locked on the action across the room, she widened her stance, allowing the attendant greater access. Almost immediately, his tongue thrust into her pussy, further exciting her.

The sway of the horse tail hanging from between Ian's clenched cheeks captured her attention. As he thrust into the blond's ass, his tail responded to the movements, swaying and jerking upright, almost like a horse in a trot. Inhaling deeply, she could smell the heady scent of male sweat and arousal.

Tightening her grip on the attendant's head, she slid her other hand between them to manipulate her clit. His nose brushed her knuckles as she plucked the tiny bud, increasing her own pleasure.

A loud moan drew her attention to Aaron in time to see him pull back, his cum splattering on *Daddy's Toy*'s face. Stroking his own cock, he jerked off until he had spurted twice more.

Kara's pussy clenched in response to the sight. The attendant was good with his tongue, but seeing the spunk dripping from *Daddy's Toy*'s face to the floor made her want a hard dick filling her.

Aaron leaned down, whispering to his stallion. Ian groaned and moments later, *Daddy's Toy* came, his milky cream splattering on the floor and the side of the table.

Out of nowhere, three more attendants silently entered the room, and Kara thrilling knowing they must have been watching her stallion in action. One moved to Aaron and knelt before him, sucking the dominant's cock. Another freed *Daddy's Toy* and licked the still trickling cum from his cock and then his face, while the third coaxed *Wandering Scotsman* away from the other stallion, stroking a moist cloth over his straining cock.

Kara could see the veins standing out in sharp contrast to his purplish-red skin. His gaze met hers. It was full of hunger for more and he silently pleaded for relief. While he watched, she ground her pussy against the attendant's face and climaxed, coating the bald man's face with her cream.

But rather than take the edge off, it only heightened her need. She leaned down and pressed a soft kiss against his lips, tasting herself, then stepping away from the bald man. She grasped a handful of Ian's mane and led him out of the stall and into the empty one next door,

Kicking the door shut, she turned to face him. "Take off the ring," she demanded as she lifted her skirt again and moved to lean over the table. The leather felt cool and slick against her heated skin and bare pubic mound.

Glancing back over her shoulder, she found that Ian had obeyed and the ring was lying at his feet. She reached between her legs and parted her pussy lips with her fingers, demanding that he come closer.

Hesitantly he complied, a questioning look in his eyes. They were both in foreign territory--had been ever since they arrived. Kara had never opened herself for him before, never assumed any kind of submissive stance.

"Mount me," she ground out, her pussy clutching in need. "Now, *Wandering Scotsman*, that was an order, not a fucking request."

The warm slide of his cock against her pussy felt so delicious she almost purred. As his head pushed into her core, the urge to purr turned into a soft scream at the intensity of the sensation.

He pounded into her, his body bent over her, his teeth nipping at her neck like a stallion would when mounting a mare. Struggling for control of the situation, she managed to command "Don't cum until I give you permission," before the ability to speak left her.

He was a stallion in rut, his body pressing her down into the padded table, holding her immobile as he savaged her. She shivered as his tail brushed the backs of her legs, his teeth clamped on the side of her neck. His hips were like pistons, unrelenting as he thrust against her, driving his cock deep into her pussy. The position shoved him in deep, deeper than normal when she rode him, and Kara thrilled in the foreign sensations of his chest against her back, the muscular warmth of his body surrounding her and he powered into her.

With a gasp, she climaxed, her body undulating beneath him. She could hear Ian's harsh breath in her ears as he fought his own orgasm.

The image of the blond impaled on her lover's cock, rosy anus spread so deliciously for his girth, filled her mind. "My ass," she gasped, her pussy still gripping his cock from the intensity of her orgasm. "Fuck my ass."

Without comment, Ian pulled out of her pussy and dropped to his knees. Kara trembled at the feel of his firm hands parting her globes, his tongue dancing around her anus before pressing deep past her tight ring.

She pushed back into the contact, wanting--needing-- more. "Now!" she demanded, uncaring if it hurt, even slightly wanting it to.

Watching *Wandering Scotsman* cover mares had never excited her as much as seeing him with *Daddy's Toy*. Even when he had ridden Aaron's little Asian mare, *Jade Empress*, hadn't turned her on as much. And then, she had whipped him while he did it, giving him a lash stroke for each thrust until she couldn't keep up with his rapid pace.

Ian shifted behind her again and she felt his cock-head press against her anus. Instinctively, she clenched as he pressed forward, then hissed at the sting. Taking a deep breath, she relaxed as she exhaled, and pushed back against him. It took some time, and tears were leaking from the corners of her eyes before he was fully seated. They were both panting from the exertions.

As he began a thrusting motion, she buried three fingers in her pussy and rolled her thumb over her clit. With her other hand, she reached back and grabbed a handful of his hair.

He pounded into her, slamming her against the table and she loved it. Moaning and screaming, whimpering and gasping, she thrilled in the animalistic rutting until her orgasm rushed up. Her pussy clenched tight on her fingers. With her last coherent thought, she told Ian "Cum when I do," then gave in to the sensations.

Euphoria crashed over her as her body was wracked with the intensity of her climax. Dimly, she was aware of Ian's groan, then the moist heat of his cum flooding her ass.

Laying her head on the table, she sought to regain control of her breathing. As soon as she could think again, she opened her eyes and turned her head. In the mirror on the wall, she could see Ian hunched over her, his body trembling as the last traces of his orgasm rushed through him.

A soft knock on the door caused his head to jerk up.

"Go away, this room's occupied," Kara called out. Ian backed away and stood watching her as she rolled over and spread her legs.

"Well, you made a mess, now clean it up," she responded to his silent question. With a smile, he dropped to his knees and buried his face against her pussy, once more relinquishing control to her--like they both preferred.

As he lapped at her swollen and battered lips, Kara draped her legs over his shoulders and fisted her hands in his hair. He neighed against her pussy in response.

BREAKFAST IN BED

Michelle Houston

Candice grinned as she imagined how excited her
boyfriend was going to be by her surprise visit. After his
company moved him halfway across the country, their
visits together had been few and far between. One
weekend a month, for the last several months was just not
working. Without telling Kurt her plans, Candice arranged
to take a week off to go and visit with him.

Catching the redeye from California, she managed to get
to Chicago at a decent hour. Carefully she unlocked his
front door and entered, closing the door softly behind her.
Slipping off her shoes, she placed them carefully beside the
door and padded barefoot down the hall. A groan coming
from the bedroom caught her off guard. For a brief
moment, she wondered if he was sick.

"Oh yeah," the muffled words broke Candice's heart.
He wasn't sick, he was with another woman. Fury welled
in her chest at how she had remained faithful, despite many
offers and here he was, banging some bimbo.

"Oh god, oh fuck yeah."

Opening the door, Candice looked in the room, her
eyes widening in shock at the lovers on the bed. Kurt
wasn't with another woman, he was with a man. A well
toned man, by what she could see. Kurt was kneeling on
the bed, his ass raised and being pumped by the man
behind him. Groaning, he thrust back into the motions,
joy written on his face. It was that look that got Candice,
she had seen it so many times as he thrust into her body or
as she sucked him to orgasm

Slamming the door open, Candice watched as Kurt and
his lover sprang apart.

Guilt flashed across Kurt's face as he looked at his
angry girlfriend. "I, um, Candice baby ..."

36

His lover glared at him, "You told me that you told her." Grabbing his clothes, Brad stormed into the bathroom, slamming the door behind him. Kurt wrapped the sheet around his waist and moved to where Candice was standing, still in shock.

Seeing him approach she snapped out of it.

"Don't you touch me. Don't come near me. Just leave me alone."

"Baby, I meant to tell you. The time just never seemed right." Running his hand through his blonde hair, Kurt collapsed on the bed, feeling his life falling apart.

"You meant to tell me that you gay, but the time never seemed right? How about when you came to visit me, instead of taking me to bed, then would have been a good time. Jesus Kurt, why didn't you tell me you are gay."

"Because I'm not gay."

Candice snorted, "Then want to explain to me why your ass was in the air as some guy thrust his cock into it a minute ago. Look Kurt, that's it. I can't handle this anymore. The long distance was bad enough, but now this? We're through."

Turning on her heel, she stalked down the hall and slammed out of the house, only to collapse on the porch swing, unsure where to go. Her cab had already left, and her shoes were inside, along with her bags. She would have to go back inside. Giving in to tears, Candice covered her eyes and cried.

* * *

"Goddamn it Kurt you lied to me" Brad yelled, feeling betrayed by his lover. "You told me that you had told her and she was ok with it, with us."

"Brad, sweetheart, please, the time was never right."

"Then why did you lie to me man? What the fuck did you have to lie to me?"

"Cause you were pushing me to tell her. And I didn't want to loose you."

"Well guess what Kurt, you just did." Grabbing his jacket from the back of the chair by the bedroom door, Brad took one last look at his lover. "I told you I don't date cheaters. And I can't stand liars."

Heading out the front door, he almost tripped over Candice's bags. Looking out the window, he saw her curled up on the porch swing, crying her eyes out. Grabbing her bags and shoes, he opened the door and carried them out to her.

"You left these inside."

Looking up at the dark-haired man, she saw instantly what had drawn Kurt to him. He was gorgeous, in a rugged, take charge way. His Wranglers hugged his trim hips, and his cowboy boots looked perfect on his tall frame.

Muttering, "thanks," Candice looked down at her hands, unsure what to do. She still needed to call a cab.

"Candice?"

Kneeling in front of her, Brad gently cupped her chin forcing her to look at him. "I'm sorry, he told me that you knew. I never meant to come between you two."

Candice looked into his light blue eyes and saw the truth of his words. "I'm Brad by the way. Just in case you need a name to put with the cursing later."

Gently, Brad wiped her eyes with his thumbs. "Can I drop you somewhere honey?"

"I have nowhere to go," she replied, fresh tears threatening to spill over. "I saved for the plane ticket here for several months. And now, I have to go and cash it in on a return ticket, which will cost me all of my spending money. I'm not even sure if I can get a flight out today, and I can't afford a hotel."

"Well, I don't see as how you have many options. Want to go back inside and call the airport? If you can get a flight, I'll drop you by there."

"I don't want to see him right now," Candice muttered, still royally pissed at Kurt.

"Me neither, trust me. He lied to me too, but I'll go inside with you. You can't sit out here alone all day."

Brad stood and reached down, clasped her hand and pulled her up. "Come on, let's get you inside, where it is at least warm." Opening the door, he reached down and grabbed her suitcases, and motioned for her to lead the way.

Once inside, she could hear Kurt moving about in the bedroom, cursing and slamming doors.

"Keep it down in there," Brad hollered and guided Candice to the living room couch.

"Brad?" Kurt asked as he came out of the bedroom, his jeans on but unbuttoned, his chest bare. "I thought that you had left."

Looking at Candice sitting on his couch, he grew more confused.

"She needs to use your phone, and you're going to stay out of her way and let her." Picking up the portable, he handed it to Candice and moved to Kurt, pushing him out of the room.

"The phone book is on the table next to you," he said over his shoulder as he herded Kurt into the bedroom.

While Candice called several airlines, trying to find a flight back to her hometown, Brad and Kurt sat down for a reasonably calm, you royally fucked up conversation. A half hour later, when Candice admitted defeat, and tapped her knuckles lightly on the door, the men had reached a somewhat agreement.

Opening the door, Brad asked Candice to have a seat on the couch, he and Kurt had talked things out and they both needed to talk to her.

* * *

He started out the conversation offering to never see Kurt again, if that was what she wanted. Candice admitted that she had enough bi friends to understand that it wouldn't stop Kurt's urges and yearning.

From there they tried their best to work things out, to move past the hurt and lies Kurt had dished them both. Sitting silently, Kurt watched Brad calm Candice down, and even begin to charm her.

Without even being aware of it, Kurt was growing aroused as fantasies of watching Brad make love to Candice and of the three of them together filled his mind.

"Isn't that right Kurt?" Brad asked. Waiting a few seconds and getting no response, he glanced over at his lover and snapped, "Kurt? Kurt!?"

"Huh?" Puzzled, Kurt focused his passion-clouded eyes on Brad.

"Have you heard a word I have said?"

Looking at Brad and then at Candice, he decided that hiding the truth would get him nowhere. "Not since you talked about staying here tonight, on the couch and Candice having the guest room."

"So you have ignored what I have said for the last ten minutes or so. Want to tell me what was so important that you tuned out on a very important conversation? Frankly dear, you about a hair away from having us both walk out of your life, for good."

"I know," Kurt nodded, his brown eyes looking like a kicked dog's.

"Will you allow me to explain?" Brad nodded and they both waited for Candice to decide. A wary look on her face, she finally nodded. Everything, all of the events of the day, the long flight, finding out her boyfriend was cheating on her with another man, the hurt and tears were all catching up to her.

"What drew me most to you Brad was the way you take charge. My job is stressful, I have to make a lot of split second decisions, and it was nice to feel like I didn't have to make any with you.

"It's kind of the same way with you Candice. Unlike most women I have dated, you know your own mind. If I don't have any suggestions for things to do, then you always do. It isn't always up to me to pick the movie, the restaurant, the sexual position."

Blushing at the last part, Candice glanced at Brad, to find him starting at her intently, watching her reaction.

"And I was thinking about what it would be like to watch you two make love, to make love with both of you at once."

Candice glanced at Brad again as Kurt's words sunk in. Shivering at the heat of his gaze, she looked at Kurt to find him looking down at his lap, a slight flush to his cheeks.

"Kurt, I can't believe that you would be thinking about something like that at a time like this."

Looking up, he met her gaze. "Why not? Given what you interrupted, given that by your outfit I would say you came here planning to jump me in bed, to be my breakfast today, how can you not think that I would think about it."

Looking down at where her coat gapped open, Candice could see where the buttons of her shirt had slipped loose. Her bra was visible, what there was to it anyways. Shifting in her skintight jeans, she admitted that maybe she had come over dressed to be breakfast, but that didn't justify it.

Brad cleared his throat and leaned back in his chair. "Actually Candice, since now in the time for confessions, I was thinking the same thing. But then again, I have known about you for a while, seen a picture of you, and imagined that since you were ok with his seeing another man, that you might be ok with joining in."

Her face flushed, Candice stood up and glared at both men. "I can't believe you two. I, I," stuttering as she became aware of the heat working its way through her body, "I need some air."

41

Moving to the sliding glass doors, she jerked them open and stepped out onto the patio, leaving the two men alone together again.

Glancing at Kurt, Brad saw the helpless look in his eyes. Sighing he stood. "I'll go and talk to her."

* * *

"You ok?"

Shivering, Candice pulled her coat tighter about her body and turned to look at Brad.

"Not really."

Moving to stand next to her, Brad leaned against the railing. "I can understand why. You must be tired after you long flight, and now this. Why don't you go and take a nap and when you wake up, we'll take you out to a nice dinner and maybe dancing or something."

"Brad look, I'm still not sure what I am going to do about me and Kurt, and while I appreciate your kindness, I'm sorry if something I have done, or something he has said has given you the impression that I am a slut. Cause I'm not."

Brad lifted a finger to her lips, silencing her stream of words. "Whoa babe, back up the wagon there. I don't think you're a slut and Kurt has never led me to believe that you are anything but a very sexy, yet oddly restrained woman. True, he told me that you know your own mind and that when in bed, you can get a bit wild. But he also told me you are a one man girl, very much believing in being faithful."

Feeling her breath against his finger was making his cock stir to life. Pulling away, he tried to be subtle about the forming attraction. "Rebuttal counselor?"

Candice had to fight the urge to raise her fingertips to her lips. The heat of his finger left her lips feeling hot.

"I want you." Flushing, Candice waited for the ground to swallow her. "I um, I mean, I want you to explain to me then why you and Kurt both seem to think that I would jump into bed with you two?"

Brad grinned and shifted, sliding his body against her. "You do want me. I can feel it with every shift of your body, every breath you took as my finger rested on your lips. I can tell it now, your pulse is racing, your breathing is shallow, and here," raising his knee against the crotch of her jeans, "You are wet. I just know it." Sliding his leg back, Brad moved away, a grin on his face.

"Now go and rest and tonight over dinner, we will talk more about why I know that you are not only going to accept that Kurt royally screwed up and forgive him, but why you are also going to let me make love to you until you are screaming for more, while at the same time trembling with exhaustion."

Her legs trembling, Candice headed to Kurt's room and closed the door. Her whole body quivered as her mind whirled in confusion. Random thoughts flowed through her as Candice stripped off her clothes and lay back on the bed.

Immediately, the scent of the two men enveloped her. Pulling the sheets over her naked body, Candice closed her eyes, trying to relax her mind. Instead, images of the two men on the bed making love filled her thoughts. The look of lust on Kurt's face as his ass was filled by cock, the way Brad's eyes closed as he thrust forward.

A change occurred in the daydream as she rolled onto her back. The two men were holding out their hands to someone. Feeling her body move, she became aware that they were motioning to her. Kneeling on the bed, she was pulled down to lie beside them, Brad kissing her breasts as her tongue mated with Kurt's.

Hearing herself moan, her eyes flew open. Her pussy ached to be filled and her nipples had hardened and were brushing against the sheets. Moving restlessly, she shivered as the cool material caressed her heated flesh. The sheet rubbed against her nipples, pulling a moan from her parted lips.

Closing her eyes, she gave in to her urges and slid a hand down her body, slipping a finger between her shaven lips, caressing the dewy flesh.

Coating her finger in her pussy juice, Candice slid it up to her clit and started to rub the tender bud. Her head rolling on the pillows, she breathed in the differing scents of the two men.

Standing in the doorway, Brad and Kurt watched as she arched into her own fingers, the sheet slipping further from her body with each caress. A moan from the bedroom had drawn their attention, and now they watched, spell bound by the seductiveness of her pleasing herself.

Rubbing her fingers faster in tiny circles over her clit, Candice trembled as her pussy clenched with her orgasm. She could for a moment almost feel a hard cock thrusting into her aching pussy, then it was gone.

Rolling to her side, she opened her eyes and saw her lover and Brad watching her. Her mind filled with images of them making love, she held out her hands to them. Kurt moved to join her, but Brad held him back.

"Candice, is this what you want?"

Smiling, Candice sat up and allowed the sheet to fully fall from her heaving breasts. Parting her lips slightly, she slid her juice-coated finger between them and sucked while looking into Brad's eyes. With a smile, he unbuttoned his shirt and tossed it onto the floor. Kurt stood in the doorway watching as Brad stripped and joined Candice on the bed. Pulling her into his arms, he nibbled at her neck.

"Now you can get undressed," he told Kurt and kissed Candice, tasting her sweet essence on her tongue. Kurt never undressed so fast in his life. Practically running across the room, he jumped onto the bed and landed with a bounce.

Candice giggled as she was reminded of a puppy that she had as a kid that did the same thing. Brad deepened the kiss, cutting off her mood to laugh.

Lying on his back, he pulled Candice to straddle him facing backwards and moved her so that she sat over his face. Licking lightly, he cleaned up her juices from her earlier play, then set to work rimming her clit with light flicks.

Kurt leaned against the headboard, his eyes glued to the scene before him. Candice's eyes closed as the black-haired man below her worked her pussy with a feverous pace. Soon he had her trembling and gasping in ecstasy. Moaning, she collapsed in his lap as her pussy quivered. Gently he rolled her over and moved back. Grasping Kurt's hand he pulled him close and shared Candice's juice with his lover, thrusting his tongue deep into his mouth.

Candice watched as they kissed, her hands beginning to run over her body again at the erotic scene before her. Never had she imagined two guys kissed to be so wonderful to see. Kurt pulled away and opened his eyes. Looking at Candice, he saw the lust in her eyes. "Forgive me?"

"No. Not yet. You hurt me Kurt, and now," she spread her thighs and gently parted her pussy lips as she spoke, "Now, lover, you can kiss me and make it all better."

Kneeling between her legs, he placed his hands over hers and gently held her lips apart, granting his tongue access into her wet core. Thrusting it in, he wiggled his tongue slightly, rubbing against her sensitive walls. "God yes lover, tongue fuck me baby. Mmmm, yes, you know what to do."

Moving to stand beside the bed, Brad had a good view of Kurt's ass as it waved in the air. Picking up a couple of pillows, he moved around to Candice and carefully lifted her to place them behind her back, elevating her slightly. Leaning down he kissed her, thrusting his tongue into her mouth, feeling her purr as his fingers lightly pinched her coral nipples.

"Want to watch me fuck him?" Brad whispered into her ear. Feeling her nod, he grinned and nipped her ear. "Good."

Reaching the nightstand, he grabbed his tube of lubricant as Candice started arching her hips into Kurt's face, grinning her pussy into his mouth. "Tongue me just like that," she gasped, quivers of orgasm racing through her body. "Don't stop you lying bitch. God don't stop."

Brad took a moment to arch a brow in shock and glance at Candice. Hearing her speak so graphically wasn't expected. Her head was thrown back against the pillows, her feeling of euphoria evident by the trembling of her body.

After sliding on a condom, Brad took a moment to stroke his hard cock as he coated the condom with lub. Moving to stand behind Kurt, he grasped his ass and quickly spread the cheeks, before ramming his hard length into the tightness of his lover's ass.

Screaming in ecstasy, Kurt squirmed forward, then slammed back again, thrusting Brad harder into his quivering ass. Thrusting his tongue into Candice with renewed vigor, he soon had her trembling and gasping and pushing him away. Her pussy almost sore, she gently stroked her clit as she watched Kurt and his lover. Brad's slim hips pumped into his lover, until he had Kurt gasping and begging to come. Looking into Candice's eyes, he invited her with a look to assist Kurt.

Quickly shifting, she slid her body under Kurt's kneeling frame and grasped his cock. Moving his dripping length against her lips, she inhaled the scent of his pre-come. Licking the head lightly, she grinned as he quivered above her.

"Please baby suck me. You do it so good baby, please," he begged as Brad pumped faster, his own orgasm approaching.

Sucking her blond lover's cock into her mouth, Candice relaxed her throat and took all of him. She wiggled her tongue against him as he moved in and out of her mouth, the force of Brad's thrusts guiding him. Sucking hard, Candice reached up and gripped his balls, feeling Brad's cock sliding against her knuckles.

"Oh Jesus baby, yes. Oh Candice, yes baby suck me. Oh my god Brad, fuck my ass." Gasping, Kurt couldn't control what he was saying. The biggest fantasy of his life was coming true, he was delirious with passion and joy.

Feeling the balls in her hand tighten, Candice pulled back just in time to feel her lover come against her face. Closing her eyes and lips, she felt the hot jets of come land on her forehead and cheeks, dribbling down into her hair. Breathing through her nose, she rode out the wave of his orgasm, feeling one of her own approaching.

Brad knew the instant Kurt orgasmed, the ass he was pumping suddenly tightened on his cock to the point he could barely move. Shifting slightly, Brad rubbed Kurt's ring with his cock until he felt his own orgasm hit. Groaning, he worked his cock in and out as much as he could in Kurt's tight ass as his come filled the condom. He could hear Candice gasping and moaning as her fingers worked in and out of her pussy, driving herself into another orgasm.

Candice moved out from under Kurt as Brad collapsed against his back. His legs gave out and Kurt slid forward on the bed, Brad's weight a familiar comfort. Gasping for breath, Brad managed to open his eyes and look at Candice.

Smiling, she stroked his back, soothing his worries away.

Finally catching his breath, Brad rolled carefully over, flopping onto his back next to Candice. Moving his hands down to his softened cock, he started to remove the condom, only to feel her hands join his. Pulling the condom off, she leaned down and tentatively licked the salty come from his cock. Her face wrinkling she glanced at him, a sheepish look on her face.

"Don't like it?" Shacking her head, she threw the condom in the bedside trash and moved between Kurt and Brad, cuddling against Brad's chest, her backside open for Kurt to spoon against as he always did after they made love.

"Not really," she admitted, tracing her fingers up and down Brad's chest. "just an acquired taste I guess."

"Mmmm, I'll have to remember that." Shifted her in his arms, he opened his mouth for Kurt's kiss. As Kurt moved back and settled into his spooning position, Brad's hand gently stroked his hair.

"So tell me honey, we made you scream, but are you exhausted yet?"

Lifting a hand to her sticky hair, Candice grinned. "In need of a shower, definitely. Sore, a bit. Exhausted? Mmmm, delightfully so." Gently caressing her side with his hand, Kurt wiggled his hips against her ass. Shivering, Candice rethought her answer.

"But if anyone is up for some fun in the shower, I might not be quite exhausted yet." Brad grinned at her answer, already feeling the need to taste her again on his lips. After all, after breakfast comes lunch.

DAWNING OF AWARENESS

Caren handed the man her money and jewelry, all the while certain that he would hurt her, even if she did cooperate. Keeping her eyes off of his face, she tried her best to make him feel secure letting her go unharmed.

"Now turn around," the thug demanded, and Caren hurried to turn away from him. A thud against her head, followed by a sharp pain were the last things she was aware of, before slipping into unconsciousness.

Twenty minutes later at the fifteenth precinct, Alex was hurrying through his paperwork so he and his partner could head home. "Hey Alex, isn't your roommate Caren Davis?" Alex nodded, looking at Antonia, the officer who had spoken.

"She was just transported to Our Lady of Mercy with a slight head injury. Seems that she was mugged or something like that." Alex stood and started to gather his things, before reality set in. He had work to finish and a boss to ask if he was going to leave early.

"Nick, I ..."

His partner cut him off. "Hey man go, I'll finish up, and I'll let chief know what happened if he asks where you are. Just make sure that you sign out." Alex tossed a thank you at his partner over his shoulder as he raced out the doors and down the hall.

Arriving at the hospital a few minutes later. He was given the standard run around until he showed them his badge and informed the nurse on duty that he was there on police business. Within minutes, a doctor was filling him in on Caren's condition.

"She sustained a slight blow to the head. We have already done several tests to rule out permanent head injury, though she does have a concussion."

Leading the way to her room, he kept talking, but Alex wasn't really hearing anything except that Caren would be ok.

Opening the door slowly, Alex peeked inside and saw Caren sitting on a hospital bed, her slender body wrapped in a sterile hospital gown.

"Hi babes," he whispered as he closed the door. "What happened?"

"Oh Alex," her eyes filled with tears at the sight of her friend. "I was so scared. He took my money, my necklace and ring. I gave it all to him willingly, hoping that he wouldn't hurt me. I never even looked at him, I was so scared if I did he would kill me." Sitting next to her on the bed, Alex wrapped his arms around her and pulled her close. Rocking slightly, he caressed her hair and did his best to comfort her.

A few minutes later, a nurse came in and shoed him out so she could help Caren dress to go home. After being allowed back in, Alex was struck temporarily dumb at the frailty of his friend. She looked so tiny, so delicate sitting there. It was more the look in her eyes than anything. The outfit, he had seen her in a dozen times, just a pair of jeans and a green turtle neck shirt.

The doctor returned and remained Caren to not fall asleep for at least another eight hours. "A concussion is nothing to play with young lady. You need to have a friend sit up with you and keep you awake. Don't try using the TV or a book."

"I'll make sure to keep her company." Alex responded before Caren could.

Turning to look at him, the doctor's face grew puzzled. "I thought that you were here to investigate the crime?"

"Several of our beat cops already did doc. I'm her roommate, and I'm here to take her home."

"Well, then, keep her awake and make sure she eats something. Not too much though, feeling too full will make her sleepy, but hunger will make her weak and more likely to doze off."

The attendant arrived with the wheelchair and Alex left to go and pull the car around. Within minutes, Caren found herself safely inside Alex's car and they were heading home.

"Are you going to call Doug," Caren whispered, worried what Doug's reaction would be. Alex was her calm roommate, Doug, his boyfriend, could be a real hot head when someone dared to mess with someone he cares about.

"Nope," Alex shook his head. "No sense in pulling him away from work. He still has several hours to go, and then he will be home. Since the hospital released you, I am guessing that you will live, so it would be better to wait." Caren nodded and scooted closer to her roommate. Snuggling against him, she felt the feeling of peace that he instilled permeate her soul.

Several hours later, she was ready to hit him. Alex had nagged, and bitched, and tickled her and any number of things to keep her awake. Caren grew steadily grumpier as tiredness settled in. She wanted to sleep and he wasn't letting her. Sure, she knew she shouldn't sleep with a concussion, but still, she was tired.

"Alex," she demanded with a whimper, "leave me alone. I just want to close my eyes for a few minutes." Caren's eyes fluttered shut again. Alex tickled her, but nothing happened. He tried yelling at her, still nothing. She seemed determined to tune him out and go to sleep. Leaning close, he did the only other thing he could think of, he shocked her.

Pressing his lips to her, he licked his tongue across their velvety softness, then slid between them to sample the wet heat of her mouth. Caren's eyes flew open. Alex was kissing her. It seemed almost unreal. A delightful curling began to take place in her belly as his assault continued.

Where before he had sought to keep her awake, that though had left his mind as soon as their lips touched. Now he was preoccupied with slowly exploring the tender recesses of her mouth.

Months of abstinence caught up to Caren, and she found herself responding to his kiss. Her arms wrapped around his neck and pulled him down with her onto the couch. Parting her legs, he shifted into the cradle of her body and tentatively ran his hands over her stomach. He knew he shouldn't be caressing her, she was his room mate and best friend, but after years of living with her, of seeing her half dressed and even a few times naked, it was all coming to a head. He wanted her. As much as he knew that he was betraying Doug, he wanted to feel her liquid heat surrounding him.

* * *

Doug bit back a curse as the cab slammed to a halt. Only two blocks to go and he hit a traffic jam. Paying the cabbie, he hopped out, planning to walk the remaining two blocks home. Tired after working all day, he really didn't want to do much other than watch a bit of TV with Alex and Caren and then take Alex to bed.

Arriving at the house they all shared, Doug opened the door, expecting to smell the delicious scent of Caren's cooking, but instead he felt like he was going to pass out. On the couch, locked in a passionate embrace, were his lover and his best friend.

"What the hell?" he gasped, struggling to breath. The occupants of the couch sprang apart. Alex stood and looked at him, his jaw flapping like a fish out of water. Caren turned a bright red, pulled her shirt back down and fled the room.

"Doug, sweetheart, I can explain."

After kicking the door closed, Dough leaned against the wall and glared at his boyfriend. "I want to know how the hell long this has been going on? Since she moved in? Is that why you fought so hard for her to live with us? Has it been years Alex?" His throat chocked up on him, Doug's voice trailed off. Tears began to fall from his blue eyes, as he looked at the only man he had ever truly loved. Alex's cock made a tent in his jeans and his soft brown eyes held a glossiness that only passion could bring.

"Doug, listen. Tonight was a fluke." Doug snorted in disbelief, but Alex continued. "Caren was mugged about six hours ago. She was knocked out, after she was terrified half to death and her necklace, the one that you gave her for Christmas, was taken. She has a concussion, and I needed to keep her awake. Now you know how she gets when she's tired. Cranky, bull headed, and eventually she begins to tune everything out. Never understood how she does that, but she does. Anyways, she closed her eyes and started to drift off.

"I have done everything tonight, cuss, yell, whine, tickle, anything I could think of to keep her awake.

"But nothing worked anymore. I made a last ditched desperate attempt that backfired. We both got caught up in it. I'm sorry love, I really am. But it happened.

"Now one of us needs to sit with Caren for two more hours, then she can sleep. I think given the circumstances that it should be you. I'm going to go and take a cold shower."

Turning away, he headed for the bedroom, not expecting Doug to move for a few minutes. Pulling his shirt off, he gasped as he felt the press of buttons and starched linen against his back. "I understand Alex. I trust you, and I believe that it happened the way that you said. It just took me by surprise is all, walking in to find you two making out."

Kissing the side of Alex's neck, Doug reached down and grasped his lover's hardened cock through his jeans. "I have to confess something. As much as I was angry and hurt, I also felt something else Alex. It aroused me, seeing you and Caren, if only for a moment. I don't think that I should go in there alone. I think that we should both go and talk to her."

Pulling away, Doug smiled. Alex was gorgeous, and watching him was always arousing. The way his chest flexed as he moved. Together they headed to Caren's room to find her throwing clothing into her suitcases, which lay open on her bed. Lifting her head at a sound in her doorway, she saw her roommates standing there and started crying again.

"I'll be out of here in a few more minutes. I'll come back for the rest of my stuff as soon as I find another place." Picking up an armload of lingerie, she dumped it into the nearest suitcase and closed it. Overflowing, it wouldn't fully close and she collapsed on her knees, still crying. Doug moved to her side and kneeled down next to her. Gently, he clasped her shoulder and pulled her against him.

"It's ok baby. I've got you. It's ok. I know what happened. I know how today happened. It's ok baby." Holding her in his arms, he rocked her slowly. Alex knelt on her other side and gently stroked her hair.

"Caren honey, look at me." Pulling away slightly from Doug, she looked at Alex and blushed as she remembered her limbs entwined with his. "What happened earlier, it's ok. It was my fault and Doug understands that. It's ok."

Leaning back into Doug, she started crying again. "I wanted it though. I have for a while now, and ..." her voice trailed off as Doug's stiffened in shock.

Holding her close, Doug struggled to rein in his own feelings. He wanted to push Caren away and tell her that Alex was his, but at the same time, he admitted to himself that he was beginning to enjoy the feel of her in his arms.

"It's ok baby," he whispered, rocking her in his arms. He wasn't sure how long he held her like that before her body started to go limp. Looking at Alex, he saw him yawning. "She asleep?" he asked.

Alex leaned to the side and gently slid Caren's long red tresses from her eyes. "Yeah," he whispered and stood. Moving behind Doug, he carefully helped him up and then moved everything from Caren's bed to the floor so that Doug could lay her down. After pulling the covers over her sleeping form, the two lovers clasped hand and left the room, a light snore drifting after them.

* * *

Several hours later, Caren slowly drifted aware, hunger pulling her from the arms of her dream lover. Opening her eyes, she glared at the red numbers of her alarm clock. Seeing that it was 3 am, she momentarily felt disoriented, until the events of her day rushed back. Swinging her legs over the side of her bed, she stood and padded silently out of the room and down the hall to the kitchen. After fixing a quick sandwich, she started to reel restless. Normally she would be sound asleep at 3 am, but after sleeping most of the evening away, she felt rested.

A soft moan drifted down the hall, followed by another. Curious, Caren walked silently back down the hall and paused outside of Alex and Doug's room, the door partially open. Her eyes soon adjusted to the lack of light and she bit back a gasp at what she saw before her. Although she knew that they were lovers, she hadn't really thought much about the particulars involved.

Alex kneeled on the bed and Doug was behind him, his sculptured hips pumping fast against his lover's ass, driving moans of pleasure from Alex. His handsome face was pressed against the pillow and his slender hands were stroking his hard cock as Doug pounded into his ass. Biting her lower lip, Caren leaned against the doorway, fascinated by the scene before her. The two men that she loved most in this world, her best friends, the secret objects of her desire, were making passionate love before her and she was powerless to turn away.

Doug groaned and pulled back, and Caren watched as a stream of come splattered onto Alex's ass. Caren moaned as she watched Doug lean down and flick his tongue against the tanned flesh of his lover's ass, licking up his own essence.

Alex turned towards the doorway, his body tensing. Doug followed his line of sight.

The light from her open bedroom door illuminated Caren to their view. Embarrassed and ashamed, she backed away from the door.

"Caren?" Doug strong voice rang out. Caren stopped and looked at him, her mouth opening and closing as she tried to force words of apology out. After the events of the afternoon, she wasn't sure what would happen with their friendship now.

"Come here." Doug commanded. Moving back, he sat on the bed next to Alex, and pulled a sheet over his lap. Alex laid down and cuddled against him, gritting his teeth at frustrated desire.

Caren hesitantly approached the bed. Looking at her roommates, she felt her pussy clench at their beauty. Each of them took great pains to keep their bodies toned, though it was easier for Alex, having a gym at the precinct.

Caren placed her hand in Doug's and allowed herself to be pulled into his lap.

"By all rights love, I should be royally pissed right now. You invaded our privacy Caren, standing their watching us. Did you enjoy it? Did it get you turned on?"

Rubbing his hand against the crotch of her pants, he felt the moist material under his fingers where she had seeped through her panties.

"Ah, it did get you hot didn't it?" Alex groaned as she whispered yes. Stretching out beside Doug, he began caressing himself under the sheets. Caren's eyes focused on the light movements.

Doug leaned down and bit her neck, bringing her attention back to him. "You just can't stop yourself can you? Are you that attracted to us?"

Caren nodded her head and leaned against him, burying her reddening face against his chest. Thought embarrassed, she still felt his hand continue to rub against her crotch.

"I love you two." Caren finally admitted.

Alex shifted against them, and sat up. Sliding a hand between them he clasped Caren's chin and forced her to look at him. His eyes locked on Doug's for a second, then he turned to Caren and gently kissed her. Closing her eyes, she decided to allow herself a moment to enjoy the sensation before she would pull away.

Carefully, Doug moved away, allowing Alex to pull Caren against him and press her body fully against his. Lying back, he pulled her with him, so that she lay stretched on top of him.

Doug shifted to lay at Alex's side, his hands caressing up and down her back as she shifted restless against Alex. Her pussy ached to be filled and right or wrong, she wanted these two men to make love to her.

Rolling them over, Alex positioned her on her back and moved down her body to remove her pants. Doug set to work unbuttoning her shirt and slipping it from her slender frame. Moments later she lay before them, bare in all of her glory, yearning to be touched. Lifting her arms to Alex. She whimpered as he kneeled between her legs and began caressing her inner thighs.

Doug moved to lay along side them, his head pillowed on her stomach, her head resting on his bent knee. Pursing his lips, he traced feather light kisses along her ribs as Alex leaned down and inhaled her scent. Parting her nether lips, Alex kissed the tender flesh of her clit, then thrust his tongue inside of her pussy. Caren gasped at the feeling of his wet mouth on her heated flesh. It had been so long,

57

and she had dreamed so many nights about him doing this very thing.

Feeling lightheaded, she turned her head to the side and opened her eyes. Doug grinned as her eyes feasted on his rapidly hardening cock. Shifting slightly, he moved against her subtly pushing his cock closer. Caren reached out a hand a grasped his pulsing length and shifted close enough to wrap her lips around his tip. Sucking tightly, she drew a groan of pleasure from Doug.

"Oh god," he muttered, rocking his hips against her face, thrusting his cock further into her mouth.

Alex continued to tease Caren, alternating between thrusting his tongue into her heat and flicking it against her clit. Trembling, she removed her mouth from Doug cock and begged one of them to make love to her. Looking up at Doug, Alex waited for his nod before moving up Caren's body. Kneeling between her legs, he paused.

"Doug," he gasped, desire making his voice rough, "Love I need help here."

Grabbing a condom from the nightstand, Doug tore the packet open. Moving to kneel beside Caren, he unrolled the latex covering over Alex's cock. Grasping his lover's cock gently, he guiding it towards Caren's pussy, and gently parted her lips with his fingertips. Thrusting deep, Alex joined his body to Caren's, moaning at the tightness of her pussy.

Doug lightly kissed her lips, exploring the recesses of her mouth, before moving back to allow Alex to do the same.

Thrusting slowly at first, Alex mimicked the motions of his body with his tongue. He was surprised as Caren began bucking under him in minutes, clenching her legs around his waist.

Moaning, she thrashed her head from side to side, ending their kiss as her orgasm crashed through her.

"Alex, oh baby yes," she exclaimed as her muscles clenched him tight.

Doug stroked his cock lightly, oddly enjoying watching his lover thrusting into his best friend. Alex groaned as Caren shifted again, moving her legs to his sides, and arched against him.

"More," she begged, her breathing returning to normal. Doug grinned at Alex's wild-eyed look.

"I don't know how much longer I can last," he gasped out as his hips started pumping faster. "I'm so close baby."

Doug moved behind Alex, and placed his hands on his hips, stopping his thrusting motions. Alex groaned and Caren whimpered in frustration. "Doug please," she begged.

Sliding one of his hands down Alex's hip, he brought it to rest at their joined flesh and began rubbing her clit in light little circles. Caren moaned as she started arching against Alex. Moving his hips against Alex's ass, Doug held him still as Caren worked herself into a frenzy on his cock. Moaning and gasping she soon climaxed, her body trembling.

Alex felt his lovers other hand gently parting his cheeks and the delightful feel of his hard cock head pressing against his anus. Sliding in slowly, he worked his head in, then thrust deep, forcing Alex deep inside of Caren. Wrapping his arm around Alex's waist, he moved his lover with him, thrusting his cock into Caren, then pulling back until once again she clenched tight on Alex's cock

As her wet heat clenched him tight, Alex could hold back no longer. His balls tightened and he felt his come fill the barrier of latex between them. As he orgasmed, his ass tightened on his lover's cock. With a muffled moan, Doug pumped faster into Alex, until moments later he joined them in ecstasy.

Collapsing on Caren's slender body, Alex tried to calm his breathing. Doug shifted to the side and flopped next to them, his softening cock leaving a trail of come on Alex's ass cheeks and hip.

"Oh god," Caren managed to exclaim, her breathing still far from normal. Nuzzling her neck, Alex couldn't help but silently agree.

Doug rolled on his side and softly kissed Caren, then Alex. Stroking his male lover's back, he commented on how sticky they all three were.

Caren grinned as she shifted again, feeling Alex's now soft cock slip from inside of her.

"I know I would love a nice hot bath," she replied and grinned. Alex flopped onto his back beside her, leaving her sandwiched between male flesh.

"No bubbles," he muttered. "I'll agree to a bath with you two, but no bubbles." Grinning at each other, Caren and Doug silently agreed to use her bubble bath and to give Alex reason to like bubble baths.

From that night one, Caren slept curled between them at night. Their differing schedules gave them all time together, and in pairs. No one ever felt left out, or unloved and as time passed, their relationship deepened into a strong, unending love, shared by all three.

DOUBLE THE PLEASURE

Erika ran her hand through her raven tresses quickly, then opened the door to her hotel room. Moans from the bedroom drew her attention and with a smile she headed to where she was certain Andrew was entertaining a lover. She had certainly given him enough time to pick up some young and willing stud.

"Hi lover," she spoke, her clipped British accent thick with passion. The sight of the two men on the bed sucking each other off was enough to moisten her panties and make her pussy ache to be filled.

"Jesus Christ!" the blonde pretty boy exclaimed as he pulled away from Andrew, certain trouble was in the air.

"Oooooh Andrew," Erika teased as she sauntered closer, her hips swaying seductively. "He is well hung. I'm surprised you could suck all that. Just imagine having it shoved up your arse." Shivering deliciously, Erika imagined that very thing. The purplish head of his cock shoved hard into her ass. Him thrusting forward, his balls slapping against the tender flesh of her ass as he pounded into her.

"Erika meet Neil. Neil, this is my lover, Erika."

Unbuttoning her shirt, she smiled at Neil, and turned to look at her lover. Lying on the bed, his hand leisurely stroking his cock, Andrew watched her weave her spell over his lover.

"So tell me stud, which one of us do you want to fuck first?" Moving her hands down to her pants, she unzipped them and slid her hand inside, teasing her clit, the crotch of her jeans tenting almost obscenely.

Neil watched her undress, a stunned expression on his face.

"I, um I think ..." his voice trailed off as Erika slipped out of her shoes and pants.

Leaving Neil standing there, his eyes glued to her body, Erika walked over to Andrew and leaned down, pressing her lips to his. Keeping one hand on his cock, Andrew moved the other to Erika's dripping pussy and slipping two fingers past her pouty lips.

"Oh fuck yeah," she gasped as her pussy clenched around his fingers. She needed a cock pounding into her, and two sounded even better. Andrew quickly removed his fingers and squirted the waiting lubricant onto his fingers. Reaching around, he shoved them up his lover's ass. Erika whimpered at the sudden stretching, even as she crawled over him like a cat in heat.

"Neil," Andrew groaned he slipped his fingers free and Erika quickly straddled him, her pussy dripping onto his thighs. "Come here and help me fuck Erika."

Neil stayed where he was for a few moments, his mind still in a daze until Andrew's words registered. Andrew wanted him to help him fuck his girlfriend.

Moving to the foot of the bed, he waited, his hand unconsciously stroking his hard cock as Erika lowered herself slowly onto Andrew's cock, then leaned forward against him, her ass perfectly displayed.

"Get over here and fuck me stud ... but don't come. I think Andrew wants that pleasure." His mouth full of Erika's breast, Andrew grunted in agreement.

Kneeling in the bed, Neil carefully straddled Andrew's legs, sliding his cock along the cleft of Erika's ass. "Stop teasing and fuck me," she growled, arching back slightly.

Pressing his head against her dainty rosebud, he gasped at how easily she opened to him. Obviously she was no stranger to anal sex.

"Yes," Erika gasped in ecstasy as both holes were filled. Shifting slightly, she could feel her lovers' cocks rubbing against each other, only a thin layer of skin separating them.

Slowly rocking back and forth, she alternated between grinding down on Andrew's cock and working Neil deep into her ass. Beneath her, Andrew nibbled on her nipples as he watched the expressions on her face. Joy, ecstasy, pain, and pleasure - they all melded into one as she worked herself into an orgasmic frenzy.

Gritting his teeth as Erika clenched him tight, Neil fought the urge to orgasm. She felt so good, so fucking tight around him. Trembling, gasping, she was perfection; a wild woman, in tune with her own needs.

"Oh YES!" she screeched like a banshee as she orgasmed, her juices trickling down Andrew's cock to his balls.

"Fuck yeah," Neil exclaimed, his balls tightening. "I'm gonna come, oh fuckkkk." Pulling back, Neil felt a brief moment of regret as his cock slipped from Erika's warm, tight ass, before Andrew gently laid his lover on her side and sat up. Gripping Neil's balls with one hand, his cock with the other, Andrew expertly jerked his lover into coming.

Milking the hot jets of passion from Neil, Andrew opened his mouth and closed his eyes, enjoying the feel of his lover's juices splattering his face and chest. Dainty hands clasped his cock as Andrew lost himself in the bliss of Neil's orgasm. Stroking fast and hard, Erika worked Andrew into an orgasm moments later.

As his come sprayed all three, Andrew groaned and collapsed against the bed, his hold on Neil pulling him with him. "Oh fuck," Neil exclaimed as his body landed on top of Andrew, their come mingling between them. Sweaty, sticky and spent, the two men grinned at each other as Erika climbed off the bed, a few drops of come working down her chest and stomach.

"I am going to take a shower now," she declared as she wiggled her hips, her juices trickling down her legs. "Anyone want to lick me clean first?"

HOUSE FOR SALE, REALTOR NOT INCLUDED

Lynn had to admit; she had never met a more striking couple than Ashley and Taylor. Both tall and sleek, one fair headed and tan, the other dark haired and creamy toned. Seeing them standing side-by-side, talking amongst themselves about the house she was showing them, Lynn indulged in watching them. The clench of their asses as they shifted, the slight brushing of their hands together, showing affection without being obvious.

Ashley turned to me as she was starting at Taylor ass, and she felt her face flaming at being caught. Being red-haired and fair skinned, she was prone to blushing at every minor embarrassment.

"Like what you see?" he asked, his voice soft and very like wet velvet running across her skin.

Shivering, Lynn replied, "Aren't I supposed to ask you that?" As his eyes flickered over her, she realized just how many ways that could be taken. "About the house I mean."

Taylor chuckled as she blushed again. His pale blue eyes rested on her face as Ashley moved around her, inspecting to see if he liked.

Standing still in a slight daze of simmering passion, she was pliant as he lifted one arm, inspecting the curves of her elbow and wrist, then let it fall limply to her side. Moving to stand behind her, his calloused hands lifted her ass checks, carefully cupping them.

"Good so far," he murmured in Lynn's ear, his face buried in her shoulder length hair. "Now about the front …"

His hands blazed a trail of heat over her body as he slid them from her ass to her waist. His fingertips wouldn't meet; it would have taken Ashley's hands as well to span her waist. "Good, you're not all bone and no flesh ... I like feeling skin and muscle, not bone."

Slipping his hands up Lynn's body, he cupped her breasts, holding their slight weight in his palms. All during his inspection, she had remained still, her gaze locked on Ashley deep simmering eyes. The man was perfect, black hair cut close to his skull, a long sleek body, deep eyes and he certainly knew how to pick clothes that hugged and accented his body perfectly.

Taylor wasn't so bad either. Feeling the heat of his body against her back was exhilarating. It had been so long since she had felt the touch of a man. Most men just didn't seem to like her slightly overweight thirty three year old body. Lynn's brains never seemed to be figured into the equation.

"What do you think Ash?"

"Hum ... I don't know Taylor. I like the way she looks, but I want to see more. I want to know what each part looks like, the coloring of her nipples is important. And is that her original hair color?"

Feeling Taylor hands unbuttoning her shirt startled Lynn out of her daze. While the fantasy of being with two men was a favorite of hers, undressing before two strangers was out of the question.

Slapping Taylor's hands away, she shifted and fled across the room.

"I, um, I think that, um," licking her lips in nervousness, Lynn re-buttoned her shirt, keeping her eyes on the two men across from her. "I think that maybe we should head back."

Ashley moved faster than she would have expected. He was across the room before Lynn had a chance to think about telling him to stop. Gently, he cupped her chin and forced my eyes to meet his. She wanted to close her eyes in spite, but instead she humored him and met his gaze. Bad idea.

Shimmering beneath the surface of a calm male was a whirlpool of passion. Here was a man who knew his own body and enjoyed using it to please others.

"I want you," he whispered, his voice threading through her body. She knew she wanted him, and his lover, but she couldn't understand what they saw in her.

"Why?" Lynn's voice trembled and she could have kicked herself. 'I shouldn't be standing here debating the issue. I couldn't go through with it anyways, so why even ask. It was time to leave and call it a day. Let someone else indulge their lusts and find them a house.'

Gently grasping her hand, he pressed it against the front of his jeans where the seam strained under the pressure of his hardened cock. "I want to thrust my cock inside of you while Taylor pumps my ass. I want to watch you suck him, licking all over his cock and balls. Most of all, I want to fuck your sweet pussy while he pumps into your ass, our cocks separated by only a thin layer of skin."

Trembling at his words, she admitted to herself the idea had appeal. It was her deepest fantasy put to words. But it couldn't be.

Her mind and her body were in disagreement. Her hand had begun caressing his cock through his jeans, toying with the hardened length. Clasping her hand, he moved it aside while his other hand unzipped his jeans, freeing his cock. Looking down at the purple crown, she felt faint.

Slowly he moved her hand back over his cock, and guided her in caressing his length. His flesh felt so smooth under her fingertips. Gripping slightly, she stroked up and down his cock, aware of what she was doing, but almost standing back and observing. She was not this person, this free spirit that would caress the cock of a man she had just met, and a client no less.

Taylor moved to stand behind her, his body hot against her back. Gently he settled Lynn into the natural cradle of his body, letting her lean back against him. "Just go with it baby, just do what feels good."

Sliding his hands over her body, he unzipped her skirt. His hands were so warm and felt so good against her bare skin. Shivering as the cool air brushed against her, Lynn snuggled deeper into the warmth of his body. By now, the whole thing was feeling a bit surreal.

Taylor's hand slipped between the silk of her panties and the expanse of her stomach. His knuckles bulged her panties out as his fingertips danced across her shaven skin.

Dipping a finger gently between Lynn's pussy lips, Taylor began to tease her clit with small circles. Ashley stepped closer, his hands moving to her blouse, as she stood there, unmoving except for her hand leisurely stroking his cock.

Baring her breasts, Ashley groaned as her hard nipples pocked against the silk and lace of her bra, begging for attention. Taylor's other hand reached out and grasped the back of Ashley's neck, pulling him tight against them, sandwiching Lynn between their two bodies as they kissed.

"She's smooth," Taylor whispered as Ashley pulled back. His words drew another moan from his lover.

"I want to see that." Moving her hand from his cock, Ashley slowly kneeled before Lynn, pulling her panties down her body. Taylor was busy removing her shirt and bra, so that within moments, she was standing naked before two dressed men. Cool air swirled around her, bringing her back to her senses. Embarrassed at what she had allowed be done to her, she flushed and tried to cover herself with her hands.

"Don't," Ashley pleaded, grasping her hands in his. Holding her hands gently, he pulled them out to her sides, baring her body to his view. Looking down at him, Lynn saw the truth in his eyes; he wanted to look at her. A strange curling sensation expanded through her stomach and chest. Warm and teasing, it left her feeling breathless. She wanted to be watched. She wanted these two men to make love to her, in daylight and to watch her, to admire her, to enjoy her body.

Leaning forward, Ashley flicked his tongue against her pussy, leaving a wet trail on her tingling skin. By now, Lynn was a mass of conflicting emotions. She still wanted to hide, but she also wanted to be free and wild, to make love with these two men.

Twisting her fingers in his hair, Lynn held him close to her, even as she gasped for him to slow down.

"I want to see you," she whispered, her face red with embarrassment. Glancing down at her breasts, her nipples hard pebbles, begging to be touched, the blush tinting her pale skin.

Arching a raven brow in delight, Taylor smiled and moved away, where she could see him. Slowly he unbuttoned his shirt and pulled it free from his jeans as Ashley delved deeper between her lips, licking her sweet juices as she squirmed.

His eyes locked on her, Taylor slipped his shirt down his arms and let it float to the floor, then kicked his shoes off. Seeing the desire boiling in her gaze, he allowed a brief smile to pass his lips. At first glance, he and Ashley had known she was simmering pool of passion and hot molten lust, carefully contained.

Reaching for his zipper, he smiled again as Lynn's eyes widened in surprise, before closing tightly. Mewling gasps escaped her lips as she arched backwards, her hands clenching in his lover's hair. Stroking his cock slowly, Taylor had to admit it was an erotic sight, his lover with his tongue buried in shaven pussy.

Ashley carefully lowered Lynn to the floor, his hands soothing her trembling flesh. "Shhh baby, it's ok," he cooed. Nibbling his way up her body, his lips and teeth weaving a sensual spell over her, Lynn relaxed to his touch. For the first time in years, she submitted herself to a lover, confident he would take care of her. Smiling giddily, she corrected herself, confident they would take care of her.

Carefully kneeling beside her, Taylor unbuttoned Ashley's shirt, smiling as his lover's cock bobbed freely with every movement.

In a well-practiced move, he rolled Ashley onto his back and pulled his shoes and jeans from him, then started playing with his lover's puckered ring. Beside them, Lynn watched, her eyes wide with enjoyment.

Twisting his head to look at her, Ashley smiled at her dazed look. "Tell me what you want," he rasped. Taylor chose that moment to lean down, his tongue rimming Ash's asshole, causing him to gasp and shudder.

"I want to watch," Lynn whispered, still shy voicing her desires.

Taylor's head came up quickly, his hair brushing Ash's balls and cook, drawing another moan from him. "Damnit Taylor."

His eyes holding hers, Taylor made Lynn clarify her statement, wanting to be certain he had head correctly.

"I want to watch you two, you know. Make love."

Smiling tenderly, Taylor leaned over Ashley, their cocks brushing together, to kiss Lynn. Thrusting his tongue into her mouth, he swallowed her moans, then pulled back.

"Feel free to look and touch," he whispered into her ear before sliding back down Ashley's body, drawing breathless moaned from his lover.

"Tease," Ashley growled as Taylor settled back between his legs, his cock throbbing with excitement. "Now kiss it and make it all better."

A devilish smile curled Taylor's lips moments before his blond head dipped, his lips wrapping around Ash's cock.

Her eyes widened in shocked glee, Lynn watched as Taylor swallowed all of Ashley's cock then started bobbing up and down, allowing a few precious inches to escape his lips before sucking them back in. 'So that is how you give a blowjob' she thought, absorbing everything she could. Her pussy clenching, she wanted more than to watch. Remembering Taylor's words, she shifted so that she was kneeling and moved over to Ashley's side. Nudging Taylor's head aside, she leaned down and took a deep breath before closing her lips over Ash's cock and sucking his deep within her velvety mouth. Tasting the heady man essence oozing from his tip as it pressed against the back of her mouth, she almost gagged, but caught herself and pulled back a bit. Taylor quickly pulled a foil packet from his jeans and sheathed his cock.

Taylor caressed her back lightly, murmuring words of encouragement and advice as she worked up and down Ashley's cock. Minutes passed, and Lynn settled into a steady rhythm. Taylor grinned at Ashley then pressed his cock-head against Ashley's ring.

Pushing forward slowly, Taylor continued to caress Lynn's back while his cock slowly disappeared into Ashley's asshole. Arching into his touch, Lynn slid her hands down to grasp Ashley's cock, holding him steady while his lover penetrated him.

Gasping in pleasure, Ashley ached to return the favor. "Lynn baby, stop. Oh God baby stop. Come here." As Lynn pulled back, his cock slipping from her lips with a muted pop, he motioned her to face Taylor and to straddle his face. Grinning in pleasure, he coaxed her into covering his lips with her moist heat, dangling her pussy before his mouth, a feast he planned to savor.

Grasping the back of Lynn's neck, Taylor pulled her toward him and pressed his lips against hers as Ash slipped his tongue past her pussy lips. Mimicking the motions of Taylor's cock in his ass, Ashley thrust and retreated, only to thrust again, harder and deeper. Within moments, Lynn was grinding her pussy against Ash's face, her thighs tickled by his stubble.

Feeling his balls tightening, Ashley knew he wouldn't last much longer. Carefully he parted Lynn's lips, his tongue dancing within her as his fingers played a quick paced symphony on her clit. Her hips bucking wildly, Lynn pulled away from Taylor and shoved her fist against her mouth. Her muted screams of pleasure filled the room, quickly followed by Ashley's grunt against her pussy as he joined her in orgasm.

Holding her carefully, Taylor pulled back, his cock bobbing with every move. Stroking the hard length, he watched as Lynn licked Ashley's come from his stomach, a treat often reserved for him.

As her head lifted, Lynn caught site of Taylor's still hard cock. "What about you?" she asked, her voice strong and confident, unlike her whispers of before. She now knew they desired her, and that it was ok to enjoy their touch.

"Well, I was hoping you two might want to suck me off now." Stripping the condom off with a quick snap, he grasped his cock in his hands and stroked slowly, waiting for her reaction.

Scooting off of Ashley's chest, she crawled towards him and pushed him onto his back. Working downward from his neck, she started nibbling down his chest, little dainty bites, enough to tease but not hurt. Occasionally she licked and sucked, but mostly she nibbled, enjoying the sense of domination over him.

"So you want us to suck your cock huh?" she purred, her voice husky with simmering passion. Looking at Ashley, she noticed he had come to rest on his stomach between Taylor's legs.

"I want his ass and balls," he stated and started licking at Taylor's cheeks. Moaning and arching against his lover's mouth, Taylor closed his eyes. Feeling the velvet heat of Lynn's mouth close over him, he gasped but kept his eyes closed. Every fiber of his being was alive and humming with desire. He could feel every breath Lynn took, every minute shift of her body.

Against his ass, Ashley was tenderly rimming him, licking his puckered star with passionate devotion. Many a night Ashley had attended to the same self-appointed chore, to both of their delights. As his lover slipped two fingers past his ring, Taylor gasped again and thrust upward, driving his cock into Lynn's mouth.

Sucking hard, Lynn enjoyed the taste of his precome as it leaked into her mouth. Salty, but sweeter than Ashley's, she knew she could easily get used to the taste.

Rolling Taylor's balls in his palm, Ashley knew just how close his lover was. Thrusting his fingers in deep, he curled them, massaging Taylor's prostate as he pumped hard and warned Lynn.

"Honey, he's about to come." For a moment Lynn debated pulled back and jacking him off, but decided she wanted to give it a try. Sucking harder, she worked her mouth up and down his cock faster and harder, milky his pre-come.

"Ohhh fuck!" Taylor gasped, giving her a last moment of warning, before his hot come filled her mouth. Momentarily gagging, she worked hard to swallow. A few drops leaked from her mouth as she pulled back, his second stream hitting her on her cheek.

Dropping her face to his thigh, she curled against him, enjoying the sounds of his orgasm, the twitches of his body. Never had a man felt more sensual to her. Smiling, she corrected herself, two men.

"I want this house." Ashley stated. Curling against Taylor's side, he pulled Lynn up against Taylor's other side. Together, they all three cuddled, a sticky mess of spent desire, and discussed the closing arrangements. Hours later, they arrived back at Lynn's office, freshly dressed and presentable and signed the papers. Several hours later they shared drinks and pizza on the living room floor, the scent of the passion still clinging to the air.

SECRET LONGINGS

Looking about him in curiosity, Kyle admitted to himself that the hooks on the walls, the chains draped across odd-looking chairs and benches felt more arousing to him than a lingerie clad woman standing next to a warm inviting bed.

As much as he tried to tell himself it was the different atmosphere, the change in setting he found exciting, he knew deep inside, what made it different. He was about to experience his deepest fantasies, his darkest desires, and his most hidden secrets. He was about to feel a man pumping into his ass; he was about to feel the sting of a paddle smacking his tender ass. He was about to explore his sexuality, in a controlled safe environment.

A quick jerk to his collar gained his attention again. Looking at his leather-clad mistress, he bit back a smile. He loved it, the outfit, the hairdo, everything. Although she wasn't beautiful in the classic sense, nor the modern anorexic model pretty, the sheer sexuality within her, the way she moved, the way she was in touch with what pleasured her was in itself sexy as hell.

Moving to stand in the center of the room, Kyle waited. He watched as his mistress attached his chain to a ring in the floor. Given its length, he could move about the room easily and even stand against the walls, but he wouldn't be able to leave the room. Not without removing the collar. He could feel the gently brush of fur against his throat with every nervous swallow. He knew he could remove the collar easily. His mistress had shown him how and made him practice it several time. He knew his safe word by heart, and could say it at will. But even knowing that, he found his pulse racing with anxiety and desire. The thrill of what was to come filled his mind.

"You are here to be my slave?" Turning quickly, Kyle couldn't find where the speaker was. Deep and commanding, the voice sent a rush of desire through his trembling body. This was it; this was the step that would make his fantasies come true.

"Yes master."

"Turn slowly, your hands behind your head, so that I may look upon my property."

Placing his unsteady hands behind his head, Kyle locked his fingers. Nervous at making a mistake, he turned very slowly, showing every inch of his body to his unseen master.

"Very good. Now stand still and bend over touching your toes, or as close as you comfortably can."

Working out every morning, Kyle knew he was in good shape. What he didn't know until that moment was how flexible he still way. Touching his toes with his fingertips, he felt a slight pull to his legs muscles, but pushed further, touching his fingertips to the hardwood floor.

A current of air brushed past his exposed ass. Kyle knew someone had come to stand behind him, he could feel it. Calloused fingers suddenly stroked his cheeks, causing him to jerk slightly.

"I said stand still slave." The sharp sting of a hand against his ass caused him to flinch slightly at sudden needles of pain, but his cock enjoyed it. Starting to harden, he felt a strange desire filling him. Different than with a woman, he didn't want the softness, he wanted it hard and raw. He craved the touch of a man, hard and unyielding.

"So how do you like your new toy?" Near his head, Kyle could smell the arousal of a woman.

"He needs a bit of work, but I think he is up to the challenge." Cupping Kyle's ass cheeks in his palms, his master gently parted them, exposing Kyle's rosy puckered ring to his view. "And I can't wait to turn his asshole into my own personal toy. To fuck it as I will."

Trailing her fingers over his shoulder and back, Kyle's mistress moved to stand beside him. Moving down his stomach, she gently grasped his hardened cock in his hand. Squeezing slightly, she smiled as it jumped in her hand. "And I can't wait 'til I get to turn him into a living dildo."

"Stand up straight." Kyle stood, his body welcoming the change in stance. Although fit, he wasn't used to bending over for so long. Looking at his master for the first time, he admitted the man was just what he wanted. His looks didn't matter as much as his presence. And master oozed a commanding presence.

"Say my name slave. Say Master Aaron."

"Master Aaron," he repeated, his voice cracking with growing excitement.

"Kneel my pet." Jerking slightly on the chain, his mistress assisted Kyle in kneeling before his master. The hardwood floor felt strangely warm beneath his legs. Settling his weight, Kyle waited for his next command.

"Your mistress wonders about your abilities as a dildo. I think you should show her how good of a dildo your tongue really is."

His body tingling, Kyle extended his tongue and held it firm, showing how hard and long he could make it.

Her voice soft, Kyle's mistress stroked his hair as she commanded him. "Flick your tongue my pet, flick it as fast as you can."

"Yes Mistress Coral." Flicking his tongue like he was licking a pussy, Kyle kept up the motion for a few moments until Coral commanded him to stop.

"Wouldn't want to tire you out yet, now would we." Slowly she turned and moved towards a strange chair. At its base was a bench, almost like a footrest, except larger. Sitting herself in the chair, she crooked her finger at Kyle.

"Come here my pet." Moving to stand, Kyle felt Masters hand against his shoulder, holding him down.

"Crawl to her, like the bitch in heat that you are."

Placing his hands against the warm floors, Kyle started to crawl towards her. A high whistle sounded in the air a moment before a sharp sting raced through his ass. "Faster," Aaron commanded.

Picking up his pace, Kyle felt the smack of the paddle against his ass twice more as he moved across the room.

"Lay over the bench," Mistress commanded him. Carefully placing himself over the bench, he found it was attached to the chair by narrow slats that cradled his arms perfectly.

Sliding down in the chair, Coral draped her legs over his shoulders, her crotch inches from his face. The leather outfit she was in was perfectly made for wearing and sex. A slit was cut into the crotch, allowing full access to her pussy and her nipples peeked out from holes cut into her top.

Kyle's knees settled against the padding at the base of the bench. His whole body was held perfectly comfortable, despite the odd position.

Reaching out her hands, his Mistress pulled Kyle a bit further forward, pressing his face into her smooth pussy. "Now lick me good slave, or you won't be able to come."

Leaning forward, Kyle tentatively licked the outer edges of her lips, tasting her juices. Intoxicated by the sweet yet tart taste, he dived deeper, thrusting his tongue between her lips. Flicking it lightly against her pussy walls, Kyle tentatively thrust it deeper, trying to learn her needs.

A sharp smack landed against his ass. "Deeper bitch, she likes it deeper." Aaron settled behind Kyle, his paddle raining soft blows against the steadily reddening cheeks of Kyle's ass. Squirming against the bench, Kyle couldn't decide what he liked better, the pussy before him or the sting of his ass being paddled. His cock throbbed for attention, jerking with every swing of the paddle.

"That's it bitch, you're a good pussy slave now aren't you." With his master behind him, taunting him with insults and praise, Kyle found his senses whirling. This was what he had wanted, the total lose of control, of being in change. He wanted the strength of another man, the will being exerted over him. He wanted to be a fuck toy, used and abused by his master and mistress.

His ass stinging, he arched his back, offering the red flesh to his master. Chuckling, Aaron smacked his ass again.

Mistress Coral withered in her chair, her body bombarded with exquisite sensation. Her eyes feasted on the show before her, her newest slave eating her quivering pussy while her lover paddled his ass. Pinching her nipples, she squirmed again as her orgasm hit. Grinding her pussy against Kyle's face, she trembled as the shockwave slowly washed through her body.

For just a moment her eyes closed.

Lapping at the sweet nectar of her pussy, Kyle was in a state of ecstasy. Even though it wasn't him orgasming, he felt it racing through his body. Every tremor of her flesh echoed through his. Quivering against her, he worked his tongue against her clit, trying to prolong the pleasure for them both.

So focused was he on his task, he didn't at first feel the warm liquid sliding down his crack. It wasn't until Aaron's hands parted his cheeks that he was aware of anything but the delightful sting in his ass cheeks. Thrusting a lubricated finger into Kyle's ass, his master smiled as how tight it was.

Kyle squirmed in slight pain as a second finger entered his virgin hole. His body was amass with confliction sensations. At one end, a tight wet pussy was gushing against his lips, the sweet smell of feminine flesh assaulting his nose. At the other end pain, pleasant and teasingly, treaded through his ass cheeks. And a new sensation, a stretching pressure as his ass ring expanded for his master's fingers.

"Relax bitch, don't you want this, to feel my cock filling your ass? Isn't that why you're here?" Nodding his head, Kyle bumped his mistress' clit with his nose, drawing a moan from her lips. A smack against his ass was his reward.

His muscle loosed in surprise and delight, his ass accepted his master's fingers easier, allowing three to gain entrance. Thrusting them slowly in and out of his slave's ass, Aaron delighted at the feel of the virgin hole clenching his fingers. He loved to breach new territory, as much as he loved being fucked by Coral afterwards.

Coral opened her eyes at Aaron's words. She knew he was close to taking Kyle's virginity and she didn't want to miss a thing.

"Enough my pet. You can stop now." Pushing Kyle's face away from her pussy, she settled him so that he lay with his cheek against her leg.

Aaron pulled his fingers from Kyle's ass, watching as his ring contracted to almost its normal tightness. Smiling, he unzipped his pants, freeing his hard cock from its confines. Grabbing a condom from his pocket, he rolled the latex covering over his hard flesh and coated it quickly with a liberal amount of lubrication. Pressing the tube against Kyle's hole, he made sure he was well lubed.

While his master prepared his ass, Kyle's mistress was gently soothing his sweat soaked hair from his face. Her touch was tender and soothing, a complete contrast to his master's determined touch.

Pressing his fingers against Kyle's ring, Aaron gently parted him again, then guided his cock head to press against the virgin hole. Pushing forward slowly, he watched as his cock head slipped past Kyle's ring. Listening for any sound of pound, and sign that Kyle wanted him to stop, he continued to push forward until his head slipped past Kyle's ring.

His patience rewarded, Aaron started to thrust softly, pushing in another half inch with each forward motion. Soon his balls slapped against Kyle's flesh, the sound masked by the groans of pleasure coming from both men.

Dipping her fingers into her pussy, Coral watched as her lover pumped into Kyle's ass. Her ears rung with their sound of mutual pleasure. Aaron looked up and their eyes met. The lust was clear in his gaze. He watched as she fingered her quivering pussy, then pulled back, pulling his cock almost completely free of Kyle's ass. Smacking the still reddened flesh, he commanded him, "Lick your mistress bitch. You're not to come unless she does. Her pleasure for yours." Smacking him again, he watched as Kyle dived into Coral's flesh, licking and sucking her pussy and clit. Pumping his hips hard against Kyle, he grunted as his cock sank all the way back in.

Pulling out, he smacked Kyle tender skin again, then thrust forward. Within a few thrusts, Aaron had fallen into a steady rhythm of smack and thrust, driving Kyle closer and closer to orgasm.

Coral whimpered as her pussy ached with need. Holding Kyle's head steady, she ground against his face, working her pussy against his tongue until waves of orgasm flooded her body. Trembling, she flopped back against the chair, small mewling sounds escaping her lips.

Watching his lover orgasm, Aaron upped his assault of Kyle's ass, pumping him harder and faster, the paddle falling unneeded to the floor. Gripping his hands around Kyle's hips, he pulled his ass back against his crotch, and fucked him hard. The bench beneath then creaked with each thrust, but neither man cared.

"You can come now," his master gritted between his teeth as Kyle withered against him. His came, spurting his hot seed against the cushion beneath him. His ass clenched tight around Aaron's cock, drawing a moan from his lips.

Collapsing against his slave's back, Aaron quickly regained his breath and moved away. Standing behind Kyle, he looked down at his slave and his lover, both wearing the same look of satisfied exhaustion. Quickly he pulled the condom from his still hard cock. His throbbing length begged for release, but he restrained the urge to stroke himself to orgasm.

Moving to stand beside Kyle, Aaron carefully removed his slave's collar and unclasped the chain from it.

"Keep this," he whispered, "and if you want to experience more, just give us a call."

Kyle nodded and slowly stood, his body trembling much like a newborn foal. Clasping the collar in his hands, he smiled at Coral, his eyes dancing with the knowledge of a pleasure more intense than any he had felt before.

Unsteady, but determined, Kyle walked across the room and stopped at the doorway. Looking back over his shoulder, he spared one last look at his mistress and master, then opened the door, once again a free man. Oddly, the feeling of freedom weighed more heavily on him, that the feel of the chain. Gripping his collar tight, he smiled and set it down on the table that held his clothes. Moments later, he was cleaned up and dressed.

Inside the room, Aaron headed to a cabinet and removed several objects then moved back to Coral. Carefully he bathed the juices of her passion from her flesh and attached a leather harness. Reaching up with smooth moves well practiced over time, he attached a collar to his neck.

Leaning over Coral, he carefully lubed the fake cock protruding from her harness and waited.

"Does my pet want to be fucked?" Grasping his cock in her hand, she smiled as it jumped with pleasure.

"Yes mistress."

WITHIN REACH

Despite the circumstances that had led up to Jared and Dorian dragging her out to the movies with them, Brenda was having a good time. Getting laid off from her job was disheartening, but neither of her best friends, and occasional fuck buddies, was willing to let it completely get her down. Alternately bullying, begging, threatening and cajoling, they had finally gotten her dressed and out the door for an afternoon on the town.

After the drama at her apartment, settling on a movie that a comedy fan, a diehard romantic and someone who just wanted to watch shit blow up was rather easy. They both compromised and settled for what she wanted to see – an action thriller with lots of special effects. Kind of light on plot and character definition, but with lots of loud booms.

Since it was a release that had been out a while, and they were at a matinee, the theater was all but deserted.

Sandwiched between the two men, Brenda found herself holding the community popcorn, and dodging dropped kernels and hand miscalculations. With each "accidental" grope of her knee and tickle to her inner thigh, she would slap the offending hand and flash a quick grin. Thirty minutes into the movie, she found herself actually glad that her friends had pulled a Neanderthal move and dragged her out of the her cave, as they all affectionately called her windowless studio apartment.

It wasn't until the popcorn bowl was settled under her seat and Dorian's hand wedged itself between her knees that Brenda wondered at the frequency of his touches. Naturally affectionate, Dorian was always pressing a quick kiss her cheek, patting her ass or quickly caressing her as they hugged. Many nights she had curled against him and watched TV until they both drifted off to sleep. Something they made out, and other they went further, but never before had just the press of his fingertips against her skin sent a jolt of awareness throughout her body.

A quick peek out of the corner of her eye found Dorian's gaze focused on the screen ahead of him, as he almost absently mindedly stroked his hand up and down her inner thigh.

Deciding to ignore the delicious tingle Dorian's touch was causing, she shifted a bit and laid her head on Jared's shoulder. Almost instantly, his arm lifted and wrapped around her shoulders, pulling her tighter into the curve of his chest. The heat of his body seduced her into shifting even closer, angling her lower body towards Dorian.

What was a warm tingle spread into a flaming inferno as Dorian's hand shifted higher, drifting up and under her skirt, his pinky brushing against the damp material covering her crotch. Squirming at the contact, she turned to look in his direction, only to find that as before, his attention seemed to be focused entirely on the screen.

Licking her suddenly dry lips, Brenda tried to subtly shift away, only to have Dorian's finger hook in the band of her panties. She could pull away and tear her panties or stay put. Deciding to wait and see exactly how far he was planning to take his game, Brenda slid further down in her seat, driving his finger against her moist lips.

Dorian reciprocated by thrusting his finger past her lips into her quivering core. Slick with her juices, her muscles clenched about the digit. Brenda tried to swallow her gasp.

She could feel him twisting his wrist under her skirt, and his finger withdrawing. Figuring he was finished with his teasing now that it has turned serious, she was about to scoot back upright in her chair when he thrust two fingers deeply into her pussy.

Brenda moaned before she could stop herself. The muscles under her shoulder bunched, as Jared shifted in his seat and raised a hand to cup her cheek. Tilting her face to his, he leaned down. His firm lips pressed against hers as Dorian pulled his fingers back and thrust again. The pad of his thumb traced over her clit while he scissored his finger back and forth inside of her.

Pulling away from Jared, Brenda moaned and clenched her thighs tight. "Guys, um, much as I appreciate your trying to cheer me up, I don't, oh god Dorian, I, um, don't really think this is the place." By the end, Brenda was panting with need. Dorian's fingers were nothing short of magical.

She mourned the loss of his fingers as he slipped them from her weeping pussy, and raised the glistening digits to his lips and sucked on one. With a wet pop, he slid the finger from his mouth.

"Delicious."

A teasing grin lit up his face as he offered his other moist finger to Jared, who didn't even hesitate before sucking the tip into his mouth.

Wedged between them, Brenda could only watch as the lovers shared her essence, both seeming to enjoy the taste as much as she was enjoying watching them.

The other couple in the theater didn't seem to have a clue what had gone on. Over halfway up the theater, they seemed lost in the movie.

Taking a deep breath, and hoping she wasn't going to find her ass in jail before the evening was over, Brenda turned to Jared and pulled Dorian's finger from his mouth.

"I, um, I ..." Now that his deep gaze was focused on her, she couldn't go through with it. "Never mind."

"Want something?" Dorian slid down in his seat, his knees pressed against the seat in front of him. With deft movements, he unzipped his fly and pulled his cock free. Brenda's mouth watered as she watched his firm hand slid up and down his engorged flesh. She wanted to suck him into her mouth, tonguing his glans as she milked his cock.

"Slid onto his lap baby," Jared whispered in her ear. Tempted, she still worried about the other couple.

"Don't worry baby. Just slip over there and lean back."

Before she had a chance to talk herself fully out of it, Brenda climbed onto Dorian's lap and slid down. Pressed against him, she almost completely hid him from view. Jared's nimble fingers quickly tore open a condom wrapper, sheathed his boyfriend's cock and guided it into her wet pussy.

With a upward thrust, Dorian joined their flesh intimately, his cock buried to the balls within her. Unable to move, she tried clenching him tight with her inner walls, anything to get the friction her body was craving.

Dorian's hands gripped her hips, holding her immobile. "Stay still." Working together, Jared and Dorian spread her fully open and draped her legs on the outsides of Dorian's.

Quickly, Jared stood, stepped over their right legs and wedged himself between their parted legs.

Limber for his height, he fit in the space, if tightly. His shoulders pressed Dorian's legs wider as he leaned down and pressed his face into her crotch.

Instantly breathless, Brenda tightened her pussy around Dorian's cock while his lover tongued her clit. Her fingers slid through Jared's long tresses as he nipped and licked at her creaming cunt.

Several loud explosions on the screen drowned out her gasps and moans as Dorian started to rock gently in the seat, driving his cock subtly in and out of her gripping heat. Teased to the point of distraction, she quit caring if the other couple knew what they were doing. They could have been standing there watching and she wouldn't have been able to stop.

Gasping softly, she orgasmed. Jared continued to lap at her spread flesh.

"Oh god Jared," she whimpered, her body convulsing in shivers of ecstasy. Tightening her grip on his hair, she ground his face into her pussy as she orgasmed again.

Dorian grunted softly in her ear.

With deft movements, Jared shifted back into his seat and wiped his face with a napkin. Just then, the credits started to roll and the lights brightened. Hurrying to pull down her skirt and shift back into her seat, Brenda caught Dorian's movements out the corner of her eye. She pulled the condom from his limp cock, tossed it into the empty popcorn bowl and tucked his cock back into his pants.

By the time the other couple strolled up the aisle, they were all presentable.

Arms around her two friends, Brenda led them from the theater to the parking lot. As she was about to slide into the front seat, Jared gave her a soft push, tumbling her into the back. Tossing his keys at Dorian, he followed her, his pants already halfway unbuttoned.

"My turn," he drawled softly, then pulled her towards him for a kiss.

Michelle Houston

PART 2:

When a woman loves a man …

and another woman

EXPOSED

Sabrina was shameless and she knew it. She went after what she wanted with a single-minded determination, and she delighted in pushing society's limits, in seeing what exactly she could get away with. Her ex-boyfriend, Julian, used to assist her in attaining her adrenalin-based orgasms. Now that Julian was out of the picture, she found herself feeling lost. She wasn't sure which way to go in order to recreate the highs she'd previously enjoyed. She was hesitant about starting all over.

The last date with her ex had ended with a blowjob during a movie, and she still had the gum stain on her old jeans to prove it. She grinned to herself, remembering the look on the faces of the couple seated in the row in front of them as the lights had come on. When they stood to leave, she was licking cum from the corner of her mouth, and her shirt sported a telltale trail right down the center. Head held high, she had exited the theater, uncaring of the snide whispers behind her.

Julian hadn't been so uncaring. In the car and back at his apartment, they had fought over the way she flaunted their liaisons, instead of trying to be discreet. The goal, in his eyes, was to carefully tempt fate, but to always do their best not to get caught. Sabrina's opinion differed. She was out to have fun and enjoy the rush of playing in public. She loved to masturbate while being watched; it didn't matter if it was by a lover, or in front of a window with the possibility of a complete stranger watching. She wanted to walk the fine line between exhibitionism and indecent exposure.

As she sorted through her closet, trying to decide what outfit she wanted to wear for her manhunt, she remembered her illicit encounters with Julian. Things had started out innocently enough, a quick fuck in the backseat of a parked car in a Wal-Mart parking lot. From there, they'd moved on to quickies in café bathrooms, masturbating one another under a dinner table in a crowded restaurant and other such forbidden delights. She recalled one of her favorite encounters, where he'd bend her over a chair in a dressing room at an upscale lingerie store and pounded her into a quivering orgasm. Trying to keep quiet had been almost impossible, but somehow she'd managed it.

Still thinking of erotic exposure, she decided on a simple short black skirt, and a white tank top worn under a white see-through blouse. After sorting through her panties, she decided to go without. She knew that when she danced, she would occasionally reveal a glimpse of her shaven pussy and smooth ass-cheeks. The idea alone was a turn on, and a sensual shiver raced through her. She couldn't wait. A pair of black and white high heels completed the look.

With the outfit picked out, Sabrina moved across the room to the bathroom and headed for a shower. After meticulously fixing her hair, and applying makeup, she was ready to go.

* * *

Half an hour later, her body perfectly adorned, Sabrina stood outside the newest nightclub in town. She'd heard rumors about the club being racy, but hadn't sampled it for herself. Tired of her battery-operated boyfriend, she was ready to find a real live cock.

The bouncer pointed his finger at her and beckoned her over. Sabrina stepped up and smiled at the muscular man and held out her ID. A quick hand-stamp later and she was inside, the throbbing beat of techno-music enveloping her.

Brushing past the gyrating bodies on the dance floor, she headed to the bar and ordered a Sex on the Beach.

After setting her money on the glass counter, she accepted her drink and turned her back on the bartender. She sipped her pinkish-orange drink and scanned the crowd. Women wore as little as possible and by the lust-filled looks of the men, she could definitely tell that a lot of people were going to get lucky by night's end. She hoped that she'd be one of them.

After finishing her drink, she set the empty glass on the polished surface of the bar. She winked to the bartender and sauntered off. Mingling with the crowd, she gave in to the music. It didn't matter that she didn't have a partner; the whole dance floor seemed to be an orgy of motion.

Catching the eye of a pretty blonde, Sabrina smiled and received a nod in return. Sabrina stepped closer toward the blonde's date and brushed against his back while he ground against his petite partner. In a smooth motion, he turned and slid a well-muscled, jean-clad thigh between hers. His hands settled on her hips and he pulled her against him, groin to groin.

Desire raced through her veins.

His body tightened against hers. Her skirt shifted, offering him a glimpse of her bare thigh. His eyes widened when she pulled back. Sabrina saw his partner's hands running over his chest.

Sabrina shifted away, turning to press her crotch against the backside of the tall redhead next to her. A feminine hand reached back and pulled her closer, squeezing her ass. Sabrina doubted that this woman cared about who she was or what she looked like. All that mattered was the feel of flesh against flesh.

The song changed and Sabrina lost herself in the beat. The blond and her date were but a faint memory, as Sabrina danced with her new partner. The redhead in front of her stayed with her, guiding her, arousing her, now dancing face to face. A faint whiff of cologne surrounded her a moment before a male form pressed against her.

Tipping her head back, she caught a glimpse of sparkling blue eyes and a dimple set in a handsome face.

His hands settled on her hips, pulling her back against him. They moved her with them; the man grinding against Sabrina, holding her pressed between him and his partner, while she ground their fronts together. Breasts rubbed together beneath the thin materials covering them both. Sabrina saw the dark outline of her partner' s nipples against her white shirt.

Behind, the man leaned down, as the redhead rose on her toes. Right next to her ear, their lips met, and out of the corner of her eye, Sabrina watched their tongues dueling. Unable to help herself, she leaned in and joined them in a sensual three-way kiss. The man behind her pulled away, leaving her tongue to play against the redhead's. He ran his hands over Sabrina's body, and when he pinched her nipples, Sabrina gasped and started to pull away.

"Relax." His deep voice sounded close against her ear. He nibbled her earlobe, gently pulling on her earring. His warm, moist lips gently traced down her neck, as all around them, couples danced to the throbbing beat of the music.

"I'm Michael, and my girlfriend's Kathleen."

Tilting her head back, Sabrina offered her neck to Michael, as Kathleen's hands skimmed her stomach and hips. Occasionally, her hands would brush over Michael's, only to continue on.

"I'm Sabrina." Even to her ears, her voice sounded husky and breathless.

As his girlfriend caressed her, Michael held her steady with one hand, while the other was busy slipping beneath the waistband of her skirt. He brushed against the silky skin of her stomach; his calloused hand tickled her sensitive flesh.

"Nice to meet you," he responded as his hand slipped down further, brushing against her smooth shaven nether lips. Sabrina trembled and fought the urge to giggle. What an introduction! There were at least fifty people on the dance floor and another fifty at tables or the bar, but she allowed Michael to slip his finger past her lips and into her quivering pussy. This was what she had been looking for.

Closing her eyes, she leaned against him, her body continuing to sway to the music even as his finger nudged further within her, soon to be joined by another. The pad of his thumb grazed her clit, and a shiver raced down her spine at his intimate touch.

A couple bumped against them, temporarily jerking Michael out of his motions, but soon he fell back into his rhythm. Sabrina didn't mind the interruption; it added to her thrill, to the hidden exhibitionism, to the risk of being caught.

When she opened her eyes, she met Kathleen's gaze. Full lips parted, she leaned forward and pressed them against Sabrina's.

One song faded into another, as Michael manipulated her trembling flesh, and Kathleen mimicked his motions with her tongue, until gasping into Kathleen's mouth, Sabrina climaxed. Orgasmic sensations rushed through her, and she felt her pussy juices coating her inner thighs. Rubbing her legs together, she trapped Michael's hand. His grip on her hip and his finger buried within her were all that kept Sabrina from sliding to the floor. She leaned her head against Michael's chest and focused on breathing. As his fingers slipped from within her, she trembled again. Fire flamed throughout her, igniting her erogenous zones.

She wanted more.

She turned in Michael's arms, her mouth seeking his. Kathleen pressed herself against Sabrina's back, her nipples like hard little pebbles. She heard Kathleen sucking on something, and turned her gaze. She saw it was Michael's fingers, her juices glistening on them in the muted light.

"I want you," Sabrina whispered, twisting her arms around Michael's neck. "I want to fuck you both."

Looking into his eyes, she saw his answer shining in the blue depths.

"We rented a room for our trip to town. It has a balcony." He paused and smiled. He slid his hands to her hips and further, fisting in the material of her skirt. Swaying slightly, he worked the material up in the front, pressing her bare pussy against the front of his jeans. The rough denim tickled and teased her painfully aroused flesh. Sabrina felt her nether lips parting, pressing her aching clit against his zipper. With sharp thrusts, Michael ground his groin against hers, never stepping back far enough to bare her skin to others.

"Yes. But only if you fuck me while I'm leaning over it, looking into the street."

Kathleen's hands shifted around her hips, pausing to rub her clit in small circles for a moment, enough to make her gasp in arousal, before smoothing her skirt back down.

"Agreed."

* * *

On the cab ride to the hotel, Sabrina sat wedged between her new lovers, as they teased her dripping flesh—all under the watchful gaze of the cabbie in the rearview mirror. Sabrina could tell that he knew something was going on in the back of the cab, but that he didn't know for sure just what. Her new friends made certain that every inch of her was properly covered, even as their fingers danced over her nipples and clit, driving her to the edge of orgasm, only to back off then start again. The ride to the hotel, and the subsequent trip across the lobby to the elevator, were some of the longest minutes of her life.

As she stepped into the elevator, she thought about her earlier self-revelation. She was shameless, and loving every minute of it. She knew that once she stepped into their room, things would move along fast. Within minutes, Michael would be sporting a condom and pounding into her drenched pussy as she gripped the balcony ledge. She wasn't sure what Kathleen would be doing, but she hoped the luscious redhead would be kneeling down, licking Sabrina's nether lips.

The elevator stopped on their floor. The metal doors parted with a soft whoosh. Gripping Michael's hand with her right and Kathleen's with her left, Sabrina stepped out and embraced the new adventures that awaited. Behind her, a middle-aged gentleman stared. She felt his admiring gaze.

Sabrina tugged on her lovers' hands, pausing their walk for a moment. She let go of Michael and Kathleen's fingers. Turning to look over her shoulder, she winked at the gentleman and bent over, exposing the edges of her smooth ass-cheeks. Her glistening pussy lips were barely visible. She heard his sharp exclamation as the doors closed, blocking him from a further view. Grinning, Sabrina continued walking, her newfound lovers laughing beside her. Yes indeed, she was completely shameless.

And for the night at least, she had found kindred spirits.

Michelle Houston

SPANKOLOGY 101

Angela Jenson
Composition 2

Composition Assignment 1:
Letter of Goals for the School Year

Professor Hadly,

You asked for our first paper of the semester for us to write a letter of what we want to get out of the school year. I want to get the most out of each class that is possible. I want to keep myself on the path that will lead to a successful career.

I want ...

I want to fuck my roommate's boyfriend until I can't walk to your class tomorrow, after I spank him like my roommate is doing RIGHT NOW."

Shit! I hurriedly deleted that last bit before I accidentally kept it as part of my paper. Then I gave up working on the assignment, since I wasn't able to concentrate anyway. Turning from my monitor to the couple across the room, I tampered down the stirrings of jealousy I was feeling.

Watching my roommate, with her lover bent over her lap, spanking his bare ass with a hairbrush, I barely resisted the urge to slid a hand down my pants and finger my clit. Ever since the night I had come home early from work to find him tied to her desk chair and Janelle spread out naked before him on her desk like the raven-haired buffet that he was feasting on, they had stopped hiding their bedroom antics. Like nothing was happening, I had nonchalantly settled myself in bed and tried to sleep.

After that, Janelle knew I could handle their relationship and that was enough for her. I guess it never entered her mind that despite being turned on by their exhibitionism, that I was a bit jealous, too. Then there was the fact that hearing the not so subtle sounds of Janelle and Terence screwing in the dark was a lot different that watching her slender hand land blow after blow across his ass with a hairbrush.

I wish I could find a guy willing to take a spanking from me, but it just never worked out. Most of the guys I dated long enough to confess a desire to spank had simply humored me, expecting a few light smacks. For the others, they couldn't get past my diminutive five foot two height long enough to let me control anything. Although several of them had been more than willing to spank my ass all rosy for me, then fuck me silly.

Janelle landed a particularly hard blow and I couldn't help but wince as Terence grunted. Maybe there was something to be said for dating a jock. Janelle landed another hard blow, and this time it was me that moaned as his rich chocolate colored ass lifted, silently begging for more. Oh, how I wanted to give it to him too.

I couldn't help the muffled groan that escaped at the idea of Terence's smooth dark ass raised in supplication while I smacked my bare hand against it. The mental image was enough to send shivers down my spine.

"You ok?" Janelle asked. Since Terence was sporting a big red, brand new ball gag, I figured the question was for me.

"Fine, although I think maybe I should leave you two alone." I wanted to be snide and add, *since I'm not able to get any studying done anyway*, but that would come off as me being a jealous bitch. After sharing my bedroom with three younger sisters, I could handle the background noise, if it weren't so tantalizing.

If only my parents knew just what I am learning in college.

A soft yelp drew my attention back to the couple across the room. Since the sound couldn't have come from the gagged football player, I couldn't help but wonder what he had done to make Janelle yelp.

"Angela, come here a minute." Sighing softly, and hoping like hell she wouldn't be able to smell my arousal, I got up and crossed the tiny room. Despite having seen Janelle changing clothes, and thus completely naked before, her bare breasts with their coral nipples still drew my attention. Despite her goth hair, she was definitely cheerleader material, with her pixie face, almost perfect body and mile long legs. Although, given how good she looked in a leather corset, I was tempted to start a campaign to change their uniform from cotton to leather. Janelle gave Terence's shoulder a gentle nudge and he moved back, kneeling beside her chair. With sure movements, she removed the ball gag.

Pointing at the bed, she quietly demanded he lay across it. When he moved to comply, her steady gaze then turned to me. I could easily drown in her green eyes; they were so full of life and fire. Her very personality and zest shined brightly through, no matter what she was doing.

And I knew the picture I had to present to her: tousled wet hair, thanks to my morning swim routine, milky white face bare of makeup, multi-colored hair, baggy khaki pants and an even baggier white button up shirt, with a black bra on underneath. Next to her perfect hair and makeup, I was a train wreck of mismatched clothes, given my habit of tossing on whatever was at hand.

She held up the hairbrush and offered it to me, handle first. "Give him a good one."

I tried to laugh, but nothing came out. *She can't be serious.* He was her boyfriend, and while spanking him in front of me was one thing, this was totally different.

"Go on." She pressed the hairbrush into my palm, forcing me to take it. Standing up, she moved around behind me, her breasts brushing against the thin material covering my back. Except for a thin band where my bra rested, there was nothing between her and me except well-worn cotton.

"Janelle, I ..."

Her hands settled on my hips, coaxing me forward, towards Terence's deliciously raised ass.

"Go on."

I stepped closer and raised the brush. I swung downward, the brush landing with a soft smack.

"No, no, no. Harder." Her hand settled over mine and together we swung. *SMACK!*

"Yes! That's it Angela. Again."

Palm sweating, I tightened my grip and swung again. The brush landed against his flesh with a loud crack. My pussy clenched. My head swam as I watched Terence jerk forward then arch back again, silently begging for more. And I wanted to give more to him. So I did. *SMACK!*

Spanking him felt so good. Janelle pressed tighter against me, moving with every twitch I made. I smacked him again, and watched his asshole pucker.

The rush was absolutely amazing. I was hot, needy and loving every tiny tremor that shook Terence's body. He wanted it, craved what I was giving to him, and I needed to give it to him.

I was so wrapped up in what I was doing, that I almost forgot Janelle, until I felt her slowly lifting my shirt.

"What ..." I began to ask what she was doing, but she cut me off, pressing a manicured fingertip against my lips.

"Just relax. Spank him again."

Her cool hands slid around my rib cage, brushing lightly over my skin, her movements unthreatening. I could feel the hard pebbles of her nipples against my back with each breath she took.

Looking back to Terence's ass, I couldn't resist. I smacked him again, and again. Fingertips moved up under my bra to my breast, tweaking my nipples with each swing. I was drugged by the sweet euphoria. His ass, so rich, sweet and dark, lifting to each punishing blow I landed against it.

My pussy quivered and instinctively I answered its call. Slipping a hand between the waistband of my khakis and my skin, I slid it down until it brushed against my clit. Circling the tiny bud, I worked myself into a frenzy of erotic motion.

Janelle's hands were just as busy, her long fingernails pinching my nipples, sending tingles of pain straight to my pussy.

I was almost there, tiny tremors heralding the wave to come. I was ready to slide to the floor, a pool of wanton need. Just one more, I needed just one more.

SMACK!

I tossed the brush on the bed, closed my eyes and leaned back into Janelle's touch, letting her pinch and play with my nipples. Her lips pressed soft kisses against my neck and ear as I slid my other hand into my pants, thrusting two fingers into my cunt as I plucked and manipulated my clit.

Oh sweet God, I needed this. The soft touch of the painted red fingertips of one of her hands sliding down my stomach should have startled me, but something about her touch excited me further, and I relaxed deeper into her warmth as she gently pushed my fingers away from my clit. Like a conductor, she was controlling the symphony of my orgasm, and in that moment, I was more than willing to let her. Her long nail flicked over my clit, teasing the sensitive bundle of nervies.

My pussy clenched around my fingers, juices already coating them. Thrusting in and out, I knew my pants tented obscenely in the front but I didn't care. Between her touch and my own, I was on the edge of orgasm, barely hanging on.

At some point after I tossed the brush aside Terence must have rolled over, because when I opened my eyes, I met his knowing gaze. Deep, dark brown, his eyes were almost mesmerizing for the sensual knowledge they held.

Trailing my gaze down his body, I couldn't help but admire his defined, firm contours. Not only had football toughened him up, but he also had the look of someone who swam and ran track. Where most serious football players had bulging muscle, his were sleeker, more defined.

I wanted him. I wanted his cock between my legs, not my own fingers. I wanted to ride his cock until I exploded, and then spank his ass while he jerked himself off. I wanted to tie him up, shove the hairbrush handle up his ass and suck him off while I fucked him with it.

Just thinking about his cock drew my gaze further down. There it was, thick, solid, rich chocolate, just waiting to be devoured. His cock-head had an angry red tint, as if he was ready to come, but was unable to.

Janelle must have sensed my interested, for after biting my earlobe gently she whispered, "He can't come 'til I let him. See that slender strip at the base of his cock? It's called a cock-ring."

I trembled with the knowledge. Two orgasms, five orgasm, ten. It didn't matter. I could ride him all day without him leaving me behind.

Janelle's hands left my body and gripped my pants. With a not so gentle tug, she pooled them at my ankles, even as my clit pulsed, needing continued stimulation. Rather than my own blunt tipped nails, it was craving a well manicured, long tip stroking over it. While I watched, Terrence tore a foil condom package and rolled the latex on his cock. I wanted to weep as his delicious length was covered, but at the same time, I could have danced for joy at what it meant.

"Go ahead Angela. Climb on."

I hesitated for the briefest of moments, running through what all of this could end up meaning, or worse, not meaning, earning me a barehanded swat across the ass. I shivered at the delicious sting.

"I said, go ahead."

Unable to resist, damn the consequences, I pulled my soaked fingers from my cunt, and wrapped them around his cock. He felt so hard, so thick. My pussy craved him.

Without giving myself time to further second-guess and doubt the moment, I straddled him. Leaning forward, I slid down onto his cock, taking him within me an inch at a time.

I felt full, stretched once he was fully seated within me, my ass settled on his thighs.

Janelle pressed a hand to my neck, pushing me to lay flush against him, when all I wanted to do was be cowgirl to his pony and ride him off into the sunset.

"Please," I whimpered. But Janelle held me pressed down. Terence's arms wrapped around my shoulders, holding me tight against his chest.

I heard the air swish, then the smacking sound of hairbrush against flesh. How had she hit him, when I was on top of him?

Then I felt it, the fire spreading through my ass. I yelped.

Again she smacked me, and I wailed her name, struggling in Terence's grip. But he held me tightly. My five-foot-two frame didn't stand a chance against his huge, muscular body.

Yet I knew if I just said no they'd let me go, but I couldn't.

Again she smacked me, and the fire spread, rushing through my ass and into my cunt. Somehow she had known. *The bitch*. The gorgeous, sexy, generous bitch.

I clenched around Terence's cock and he jerked, his chest hair brushing my nipples. She smacked me again, and the chain reaction continued.

I was helpless. I was exhilarated. The high I had felt earlier returned, mixing with the loss of control I was experiencing. It was everything and nothing, rolled into one.

And again. I was in charge; I could stop this at any moment. Until then, I was helpless, completely at their mercy.

I loved the sensations rushing through me. I gave myself up to the sweet sting and rode the wave.

I lost track of the count at ten. My pussy demanded attention. Clenching tight with each pleasurable sting, I surrendered myself to the sensations, until with a muffled scream I came, clenching Terence's cock deep within me, allowing my roommate of two years to paddle my tender ass.

I kept my face buried in his chest, gasping for air as the world tried to right itself. If it was a heartbeat later that I rolled to the side or an hour later, I really don't know.

With a knowing smile Janelle climbed onto the bed and took my place straddling Terence. Her hand was gentle as she stroked her fingers through my hair. I sat up, and pressed a soft kiss against her lips, allowing our tongues to duel for just a brief, forbidden moment before I pulled back and whispered, "Thank you."

"Any time Angela. *Any* time." She punctuated her comment by trailing her fingers down my chest to my stomach and swirling a fingertip in my belly-button before sliding just a little further down, a pixie smile on her face. Softly, delicately, her fingertips touched against my pussylips, stroking over the puffy flesh. Her gaze locked on mine, she slid a fingertip inside of my cunt, just barely an inch, then pulled it free. Holding it to her lips, she wrapped them around her creamy digit, sucking off my essence.

I nodded to show I understood and smiled back. All I wanted to do in that moment was return the favor, to slide around behind her and finger her tiny button of a clit while she rode Terrence to orgasm. But I had already surpassed my understanding of myself in that moment. Everything I thought I had known about myself, and my sexuality, had just been tossed out of out three-story dorm window.

Unable to process any more, I nodded one more, then turned away, giving them what privacy I could. Picking up my pants I pulled them on and sat back down at the computer to work on my English paper, trying my best to ignore the wetness seeping into the material.

Behind me, I could hear Janelle removing the cock ring, Terrence's moans of appreciation a symphony around me. "Now baby, since you've been *so* good."

The sound of Terence's husky groan as Janelle sank down on his cock was the second sweetest sound I had ever heard; second only to the subtle rasp of her fingernail scratching over my skin.

The bed groaned and creaked as she rode him like I fantasized about, like I knew I would one day. Maybe while I was riding him, his strong arms holding me immobile to their demands she would come up behind me and fuck me with a strap-on. Or she could have him sit in a chair, and straddle him, leaning her back into his chest, leaving room for me to kneel between their feet and lick and suck at where their flesh joined.

My inner thighs trembled at the fantasy, and I knew that I had to stop torturing myself with plans of what could be and get my damn paper written. Then, and only then, could I allow myself to play again. Turning my attention to my screen and trying my best to ignore the steady throbbing sting of my ass, I started typing.

Angela Jenson
Composition 2

Composition Assignment 1:
Letter of Goals for the School Year

Professor Hadly,
You asked for our first paper of the semester for us to write what we want to get out of the school year.

What I want most is a well-rounded education. I want to know more than books can tell me, although I do want that knowledge as well. I want to walk out of college with more than a classical education - I want to be prepared to live in the real world.

I want to leave college feeling like I truly got the most out of it. Up until now, I have been settling for just the book knowledge, immersing myself within the pages, until I have no room left for anything else. But that ends now. I want to learn what the books can't teach us. What no one has been able to put to words yet.

I want to get to know who I am, who I can be, and what I truly want out of life.

I guess, I just want it all, and I'm not going to settle for anything less anymore.

Life demands sacrifices and risks, to truly be lived. And I am ready to start living. I am ready to finally start accepting myself, my wants, needs, desires and dreams. I am ready to start finding *me*.

Michelle Houston

A LITTLE BIT OF HEAVEN

Bridgett watched Mark dance with Ivy. She knew that Mark was trying to convince Ivy to sleep with him. Correction, to sleep with them. Mark had wanted to do a threesome for a long time now, ever since she had told him she though that she might be bisexual. 'They look really good together,' she thought. Ivy's pale skin to Mark's dark tan, her light blonde hair to his sinfully dark hair. His six foot six frame to her five foot eight. 'I can even imagine what they will look like in bed together,' she thought, 'I should be able to, Mark is my husband, Ivy my lover.'

Ivy and Bridgett had met during their college biology class one day when the professor partnered then to do a lab together. Then they got to be study partners, friends, then one rainy night while Mark was out of town, lovers. Two days, and a lot of making love later, when Mark got back into town she had confessed what she had done. Mark had smiled and said it was ok, as long as it wasn't another guy he was cool with it. Since then however, he had made it very clear that he really was not adverse to a threesome. Finally Bridgett had told him the night before, just to shut him up, that if he asked Ivy and she was ok with it then they would do it.

Ivy had called a few hours ago and suggested that they go out, Mark had asked to tag along and so far Ivy didn't look displeased. Actually she appeared to be having fun with Mark. The song ended and they approached the table, laughing. Bridgett smiled at them as they sat down.

'She doesn't look to happy,' Ivy thought, 'I wonder what she really thinks of the idea of sharing her husband.' "So, Bridgett, Mark tells me that you and he were wondering if maybe we could do a threesome. Honestly how would you feel about that? I don't want to come between you and your husband, or to loose you myself."

'Oh no, now here it comes. If I say I don't want to will Mark be mad? If I say yes will I regret it?' "Honestly Ivy I don't know if I want to or not. I love Mark, I care for you, I like sex with both of you, but will I be able to handle seeing you two together? I don't know."

"Can I say something?" Mark finally decided to join the conversation. At the women's nods he continued. "Look Bridgett, I don't want you to do anything you don't want to do. I have always wanted to see another woman make love to you, not be made love to by two women myself. I would be happy to watch and just touch you."

Bridgett smiled, and she felt her heart tighten with love for Mark. 'He is so understanding,' she thought, forgetting that just moments before she had worried he would be angry. "Let's do it," she said.

Mark paid the bill while Ivy and Bridgett went and claimed the car. He climbed into the driver's side of the car and pulled away from the dance club. The ride to his and Bridgett's home was made in silence, broken only by the soothing melodies of Mozart. Ivy and Bridgett sat together in the back seat, hands clasped and pressed up against each other.

When they arrived home, Mark opened the car door for Bridgett and Ivy and helped them out of the car. Bridgett unlocked the door and stepped inside to turn some lights on. Ivy followed, suddenly unsure if she was doing the right thing. Mark came in last and closed and locked the door.

"Ivy I ..."

"Bridg ... I" The women laughed. "You first," Ivy said.

"Ivy, I think we should go upstairs and get things started and let Mark follow in a few minutes." Ivy smiled and nodded her head. They again held hands, and together that climbed the stairs and disappeared into he bedroom. Mark watched them walk away, then went into the kitchen and got himself a glass of ice cold water. Wanting for a moment to dump it on his head, he drank it instead.

Upstairs, Ivy and Bridgett were kissing and disrobing each other. They caressed and kissed each bit of flesh they uncovered. Some of the spots were ticklish which caused a lot of laughter. Ivy was sure she was doing the right thing. She cared for Bridgett and she was a exhibitionist at heart. As long as Mark did nothing more than maybe lightly touch her or some such, no actual intercourse, she would be ok. Bridgett was thinking along the same lines.

Their lips met as their nude bodies rubbed against one another. Mark leaned in the door way and watched them sway to the softly playing music they had put on. Silk's Freak Me played and the women ground their lips and pelvises together and they ran their hands up and down the other's back. Mark could feel himself growing very aroused, but stayed where he was, just enjoying the show. Ivy slowly swayed from side to side and dropped down to kneel in front of Bridgett. Mark saw her tongue flick against Bridgett's small patch of red pussy hair, then rub her pussy lips. Mark could stand no more, he entered the room and moved to stand behind Bridgett. His large hands caressed her breasts, then flicked her nipples. Bridgett moaned at their combined touch. Mark's pants began to restrict him and even to becoming a bit uncomfortable, but he left them on. Bridgett began to sway and Ivy leaned back. Mark picked her up in his arms like she weighed nothing, but then again she was only five foot five inches tall. Mark had a good foot or more in height on her, so to him, she did weight almost nothing.

Ivy followed Mark to the bed and watched him gently lay Bridgett down so that her legs dangled off of the bed. He stepped back and watched again, as Ivy once again knelt before Bridgett and began to tongue her. Bridgett thrashed her head as Ivy expert tongue drove her crazy with desire. Her hips rose slightly and she began to thrust against Ivy's tongue. Mark stripped of his clothes and climbed on the bed next to Bridgett. Ivy again stopped what she was doing and told Bridgett to slid up a bit. Then Ivy climbed over her so that they were in a sixty-nine position. She slowly lowered her bare pussy over Bridgett's face as she drive her tongue into Bridgett's pussy. Mark began to stroke his cock as he watched the sexy scene before him. His wife, with her tongue deep inside a woman pussy, her pussy filled by a woman's tongue.

A drop of pre-come rolled off of the tip of his cock as Bridgett slid a hand over his stomach and gently grabbed his cock. She slid her hand up and down in time with her tongues thrusts. Ivy joined in the fun and cupped Mark's balls. She squeezed in time to her tongue thrusts. Mark lay on the bed and moaned as he just watched the ladies make love and let them take care of him and each other.

He began to arch his hips and he grew closer to orgasm, thrusting his cock into the tight glove made by his wife's hand. Her lover gently squeezed his balls faster as she speed up her ministration to Bridgett's clit and pussy. Bridgett began to squeeze Mark cock a little tighter and he knew she was close to orgasm. Her hips arched faster into Ivy's tongue, Ivy ground her pussy down onto Bridgett's face a little bit faster. Bridgett came first, driving her tongue farther into Ivy's pussy, tasting the sweet nectar. Her hand tightened on Mark and he came, coating her hand and a small area of the bed with his semen. Ivy moaned and quit tonguing Bridgett and began to rub her pussy harder and faster over Bridgett's face. Then she came as well. Her back arched and a half moan, half scream escaped her lips.

Mark watched Ivy arch her back and smiled. His fantasy had come true and it was better than he thought it would be. He loved to watch his wife with her lover. It was arousing, it was stimulating, it was a little bit of heaven on earth.

A Not So Reluctant Hero

Michael had barely put his feet up after a long day's work when he heard the screams from Julie's room. He rushed to her aid, finding her and Susan, her girlfriend, standing naked on the bed, pointing at the floor.

His eyebrow arched as he watched the two women bouncing on the mattress, their breasts jiggling.

"Michael, spider -- kill it! Please!"

Julie was terrified, hating spiders with a passion. Obviously, so did Susan.

The crisis ended beneath Michael's shoe and with the flush of the toilet, and upon his return to the bedroom he was slightly irritated to find neither woman had yet bothered with their clothes.

Julie was pale, tall and slender; Susan was tanned, short and slender, but with well-placed curves. Two lovely, naked redheads and he couldn't touch either of them -- that was the rule set down by Julie when he moved in almost six months ago, and until today he never had any reason to challenge it.

"Michael, thank you. You're our hero," Julie said.

Susan smiling. "Nice of you to leave the white horse at the door."

Michael bit the inside of his cheek, trying not to smile. He was still mad at them ... well, sort of mad. OK, truth be told, he wasn't mad at all. He actually found himself rather amused as both women turned several shades of red, as they realized their state of undress.

He almost smiled, but his arousal was uncomfortable. He wanted so badly to reach out and caress the gentle lines of Julie's neck, or feel Susan's ample breasts in his strong hands.

Susan looked into his eyes, trying to cover herself with the comforter. Ever the gentleman, Michael turned and was leaving to allow the ladies to dress and regain their dignity, if not their normal skin tone, when a movement froze him in his tracks.

Susan had dropped the comforter and was following him to the door. He turned, and she stopped a few feet away and struck a seductive pose, thrusting her breasts upward, displaying her hard nipples and the red patch of hair on her mound.

Julie was on the bed, watching the scene unfold. She had always been attracted to guys, she simply was more attracted to women.

Michael had been the exception. Julie had wanted him from the start, but she just had not been ready to sleep with a man. Now she was, and from the way her friend was looking at him, so was Susan. No problem with Julie, since the two shared everything.

Michael slowly walked toward Susan, making certain their signals weren't crossed, not wanting to act on a mistaken impression. Susan reached out and pulled him to her, rubbing her body against his, and he knew his impression was true.

Susan's hands stroked his chest as she undid his buttons, hearing the silk shirt hit the floor with a soft swish. Her hands ran freely over his muscular chest, tweaking his nipples and twirling in his hair.

Michael grinned, then leaned down and kissed her. Julie took it all in from the bed, her legs spread as she caressed her thighs.

Susan slid Michael's pants off, Julie watching as Michael's cock hardened and her friend brushed her body back and forth against him. He thrust his tongue into Susan's mouth, then pulled back, gently kissing from her mouth to her neck, lightly nipping the smooth skin of her throat to the sound of her moans.

Michael slid his hand under her ass and lifted her against him. Susan wrapped her legs around his waist and tried to drive his cock deep inside ... only he kept shifting so she couldn't impale herself.

Julie's fingers began to trace little circles on her thighs and stomach, caressing and tickling her aroused flesh. She and Susan had just been getting serious upon the untimely arrival of the late spider.

Michael's hands roamed down the back of Susan's thighs as he carried her to the bed. Gently he lay her down and came down atop her, the hair on his chest scratching her tender nipples. She squirmed, her moans soon swallowed in a kiss of pure lust.

Julie moved closer to them, kneeling beside their heads. Her hands were fondling her breasts, drawing the nipples into little hard peaks, then wandering at their soft undersides.

Susan's nipples rolled gently in Michael's strong hands, his lips leaving hers to kiss down her body. Slowly he sucked one of her hard peaks into his wet mouth, his tongue caressing it, rolling it into his mouth. She moaned and arched her back, pushing her breasts up into his face.

Julie's hands slid down her stomach to her pussy, playing with the bare mound, her fingers sliding inside, wetting them with her juices, and massaging her clit.

Michael's lips moved to Susan's pussy, his tongue licking her lips, then flicking against her clit. He met Julie's eyes as she leaned over to offer her breasts to Susan, who sucked an erect nipple into her mouth as Michael thrust his tongue inside her.

His eager hands caressed Susan's breasts as she moaned and thrashed against him and the bed, Julie's orgasm fast approaching. Susan arched her hips up into Michael's skilled tongue, craving his touch.

"He's almost as good as Julie," she thought.

She liked having his tongue inside her, but she really wanted his cock. Her hands fisted in his hair and gave a gentle tug, and Michael responded by rubbing his tongue once more against her clit, then softly exhaling against it before moving up her body again with tender kisses.

Julie leaned back and began flicking her clit faster, with greater need, her finger moving in little circles, her back arching as her orgasm began. Her moans filled the room as Michael joined his body with Susan's for the first time.

In and out, gently he thrust, Susan pushing up against him as he filled her. Soon he felt her inner muscles clenching in orgasm, her breaths short, her moans louder. Michael thrust once more, then held himself still above her.

He still hadn't come, and Julie wanted him.

Susan's breathing calmed and her nails stopped digging into his back. Michael lifted his muscular body off Susan and lay down atop Julie, his lower body between her open legs.

"What do you want?" he whispered into her ear, then he gently nibbled on it.

"You, hard, deep inside me."

Michael obliged. Slowly he slid an inch inside her. Then he pulled back. He penetrated two inches, then pulled back again.

Over and over, he slowly slid inside Julie, her body stretching to accommodate him. Finally, his patience rewarded, he bore all the way in, and Julie was a virgin no longer. Her red hair fanned on the pillow, the soft green silk sheets accenting the color.

Susan knelt where Julie had been, but this time she kissed her girlfriend as Michael thrust slowly into her, over and over. Julie's hips arched up slightly into his thrusts as she felt the full return of her desire. She caressed his back and his ass.

Susan broke the contact of her lips with Julie and kissed Michael; he then kissed Julie. His thrusts sped up and he leaned back slightly so Susan could slide a hand between their joined bodies. She caressed Julie's hard little clit as his pace increased.

The lovers' lips met again, his tongue thrusting into her mouth in rhythm with his cock sliding into her pussy. Julie's head thrashed on the pillow, her body clenched on Michael's cock as he kept thrusting, his own orgasm near.

Julie arched off the bed, Susan's finger on her clit and Michael's cock driving her over the edge. Susan smiled as she watched her friend come, and with a final thrust Michael came, too, his hot sperm pulsing from his cock deep into her pussy.

Julie's muscles relaxed as she calmed. Susan sat beside them, caressing Julie's hair and Michael's back, soothing them both for some time.

The three exchanged kisses, seemingly spent, until Julie teasingly traced Michael's lips with her tongue. She began to suck on Susan's nipples again, now lightly touching her friend's hard clit.

She felt Susan's pussy lips quiver as they always did after an orgasm, and began to massage her clit. Michael slid a hand down Julie's body, playing with her bare mound and lips.

With hands surprisingly gentle for his size and strength, Michael coaxed Julie to desire again, and into a sitting position. Susan helped Julie straddle Michael's face, and immediately Julie began to rub her wet pussy against his mouth, his tongue darting into her sex.

Susan leaned down and began to lick the tip of Michael's cock, which jerked and hardened to her touch. When it stood tall and proud she straddled his hips and slowly lowered herself onto him. Michael paced his tongue to Susan's teasing movements, and soon Susan had Michael fully inside of her, rocking back and forth on his hardness, caressing her clit.

Julie leaned forward, the two women kissing as Michael pleased them both, his tongue inside one, his cock inside the other. Susan quickly built to another orgasm as she ground her pelvis against Michael; one hand caressed her breasts, the other her clit.

Julie rubbed her tongue against her lover's as she allowed Michael's mouth to please her. Soon, Susan began to shake and moan. Their lips broke contact as Susan threw back her head and moaned, her orgasm overtaking her.

Julie's pace quickened and Michael tasted her sweetness coating his tongue and throat. It was a heady sensation, making love to two women at once, and he could hold out no longer. His balls again tightened in orgasm, and he came with a final thrust of his cock deep inside Susan, his tongue inside Julie.

Rocking her hips and caressing her clit, Julie finally orgasmed herself, trembling, the final thrust of Michael's tongue being precisely what she needed. Susan moved her body off Michael's and up higher on the bed to hold Julie. Their breasts touched and their lips met in a gentle kiss, Julie's body shaking in the aftershock of intense climax.

Susan slid Julie to the side, allowing Michael to breathe, and she noticed his satisfied grin. It pleased her to think that she and Julie had put that expression on his face.

Tenderly Michael and Susan caressed Julie's body, calming her, soothing her until finally all three of them lay cuddled together as the last rays of sunlight left the sky.

"Sometimes it pays to be a hero," Michael thought, "not that I ever would have considered myself hero material."

INTRODUCING THE LOVERS

Knocking tentatively at Ava's hotel room door, Meghan almost had time to convince herself, and to talk herself out of leaving, twice before the door opened. While dating Ava was good, she wasn't certain she was ready to take it to the next level and introduce Ava's boyfriend into their relationship. Although she and Jim had been chatting online for a while, getting to know each other, she still wasn't sure she was ready for this next step.

"Hello you," Ava drawled as she swung the door wide. "I was wondering if you had gotten lost, or changed your mind." Stepping aside, she watched as Meghan hesitantly entered.

"Meghan, I'd like to introduce Jim. Jim, my love, this is Meghan."

"Mmmm," the tall man murmured, "charmed to finally meet the woman I've been tasting for months."

Meghan blushed at Jim's words. While she was used to his teasing online, this was different. Looking at the bed, she was surprised to find him dressed and lounging against the headboard. She had expected him to be wearing a robe, or nothing. Given why she was there, it would have made sense.

"Are you ladies ready to go?"

Glancing at Ava, Meghan cocked her head to the side in confusion. "Where is he taking us?"

"To dinner. We haven't eaten today and it's almost three, so we thought a light dinner would be appropriate."

"Ok." Meghan agreed as she watched Ava grab her jacket. Dressed in all black, she looked as beautiful as ever. For his age, Jim wasn't half bad either. Just shy of forty, he looked good dressed casual in jeans and a button up shirt. On him, the look fit. He was a casual type of person, at home pretty much anywhere.

The ride down to the lobby was made in silence, as Meghan nervously twisted her hands together. Jim was nice and everything, but it had been years since she had let a man make love to her, and she just didn't know if she could go through with it. Ava had made it clear that if Meghan wasn't ready, that was ok, but she knew Ava was also dying to bring him into the mix.

Following behind Jim and Ava in a preoccupied state, she almost stumbled as Jim stopped suddenly at the door to the lodge restaurant. "This way ladies," he murmured as he grasped Ava's elbow, then turned and grasped Meghan's as well. Guiding them both to a prearranged table in the corner, he seated Meghan between him and Ava.

After taking their order, their waiter retreated to the other side of the restaurant, leaving them in peace. As early as it was, they were one of only three groups eating. Seated in the corner, behind a half-enclosure, they were guaranteed some privacy.

Nervously fiddling with her water glass, Meghan almost jumped when Jim spoke. Instead, she just gasped, then blushed deeply.

"It's ok to be nervous Meghan, but you know me. You know I'd never ask you to do anything that would make you uncomfortable.

"After dinner, if you wish, we'll retire to our room where I'd love to watch you and Ava make love. If you allowed me to, I'd indulge my fantasy of licking from the tips of your topes, to the widow's peak on your forehead. But only if you wished, otherwise I would be more than happy to just watch.

"But under no circumstances do I want you to do anything you don't want to. If, after dinner, you wish to go home, that's fine with both Ava and I."

Certain where they stood, Meghan relaxed a bit and allowed Ava and Jim to tease her into a good mood. By the time they all turned down desert, Meghan was feeling relaxed and mellow in their company, despite the thread of nervousness that still rushed through her. She knew what Jim had said was true-it was her decision.

As Jim paid the bill, Meghan decided to at least fulfill some of his fantasy, as well as her own. Grasping Ava's arm, she gently guided her to the elevator, where they waited for Jim, hands held like teenagers. Giggling at his look of shocked glee, Ava and Meghan leaned towards each other, their lips briefly brushing before the elevator doors opened. Stepping inside, Meghan leaned against the back as Ava and Jim joined her.

The doors opened and as Meghan moved to step out, Jim grasped her arm lightly, "I meant what I said. It's your call."

Nodding slightly, Meghan leaned up and pressed quick kiss to Jim's lips, inhaling his fragrance as she did so. First, the husky tone of his voice, and now this masculine, yet light, scent. She didn't know if she'd be able to stand what was ahead. All throughout dinner, her insides had been quivering with every word he spoke. Ava's voice was heavenly; Jim's was down right seductive.

"Ready?" Ava asked, her voice coming out huskier than normal. The doors closed, prompting Jim into action. Ava stood in the hotel room doorway, a smirk on her face. "You two coming or not?"

Holding out his hand, Jim waited. Placing her trembling hand in his, Meghan shivered as his hand closed over hers. Smiling, or at least trying to, her eyes met his and a wealth of information passed between them. Nodding slightly, Jim seemed to accept what her eyes said.

Leading Meghan into the bedroom, Jim backed away, allowing Ava to step against Meghan, her breasts pressing against the auburn haired woman's back. "I want you," she whispered in Meghan's ear, her teeth nipping at the tender lobe.

Sitting in the room's only chair, Jim watched as Meghan swayed in Ava's arms, eyes closed, enjoying her lover's touch.

Reaching her arms around Meghan, Ava slowly undressed her lover, turning her slightly so that Jim could see every inch of flesh as it was revealed. High, pert breasts topped with coral nipples, straining to be touched. Smooth, shaven skin, moist and glistening in the moonlight creeping through the curtains.

Relaxing into his chair, Jim watched, mesmerized as Ava slowly stroked Meghan's' flesh, her black clothing a perfect contrast to Meghan's creamy skin. Gently parting Meghan's nether lips, Ava slipped a finger deep within her pussy, drawing a gasp from her lover. Trembling, Meghan leaned back against Ava, confident she would hold her upright.

Knowing Jim watched was a turn on for Meghan. Being the focus of an almost stranger's attention, of his lust. Even though they had spent months chatting, exchanging emails, in the flesh he was a stranger to her. An unknown.

"Part your legs for me baby," Ava whispered, slipping two fingers between Meghan's lips as her other hand grasped Meghan's, drawing it up to her breasts. Together they massaged Meghan's breasts, teasing the hard nipples, as Ava's fingers thrust within her.

Opening her eyes, Meghan's gaze met Jim clouded stare. He was turned on, but restrained, waiting to see what she would allow.

Her legs trembling, Meghan stepped forward slowly, Ava staying pressed against her back. Every step brought her closer to Jim, her shaven mound on perfect eye level for him. Inhaling deeply, he seemed to Ava to be enjoying Meghan's scent. Every time he exhaled, Meghan trembled, as his breath whispered across her skin.

Pulling her fingers from Meghan's quivering flesh, Ava offered them to Jim, her breath quickening at his moan of appreciation, as he tasted her lover's sweet juices firsthand.

"I told you he'd love your taste," Ava whispered, her breath soft against Meghan neck. Placing a quick kiss, then

117

biting softly, Ava held Meghan steady as she trembled. "He loves pussy, well-tended, sweet pussy. I'd think he is a lesbian in training, if not for his delicious cock."

Jim groaned as Ava pulled her fingers back, denying him the last traces of Meghan's juices. Sliding her saliva-coated fingers down Meghan's stomach, she parted her lover's lips again, only to have her whisper no.

Swallowing hard, Meghan fought to let the words free of her lips. "I want Jim to do it," she whispered, her voice hoarse with need.

Cocking an elegant eyebrow at her, Jim slowly extended his hand, waiting to see if she would change her mind. When she slowly nodded, he allowed his fingers to trace the delicate lines of her feminine flower, to peruse the petals, moist with desire. Slipping one finger past her dewy folds, he caressed her little nub, smiling when she jumped and gasped with lust. Running his finger over her clit in tiny little circles, Jim watched every little move she made. Closing her eyes, Meghan leaned back against Ava, her lover placing little kisses along her neck as her tender fingers caressed her hard nipples.

Working a finger into her tight pussy, he switched to rubbing her clit with his thumb, the calloused pad rough against her tender flesh. Moaning, Meghan melted into his touch, her body coming alive with desire. Grinding against her back, Ava rubbed her legs together, her clit excited by the friction.

"Want to ride his face while I fuck him?" Ava taunted, her words evoking vivid images in Meghan's mind. Nodding slightly, she gasped as Ava pulled away, quickly shedding her own clothes. Meghan quivered as Jim stood, his fingers driving deeper within her. Pressing his body against her, he guided her backwards, his fingers thrusting in and out of her with every step.

Her knees bumped the edge of the bed and Jim's fingers left her. Sitting down, Meghan scooted to the center of the bed while watching Jim undress. As his cock was revealed, Ava reached out, wrapping her delicate hand around his thickness, pulling him onto the bed. Rolling together, their lips locked in a passionate embrace, they bumped up against Meghan's legs, Jim lying on his back, with Ava astride him.

Pulling her lips from his, Ava grinned and slid backward, her pussy welcoming his cock into her heat. Groaning in appreciation, Jim closed his eyes for a moment, only to open them again. as Meghan lowered her dripping pussy onto his face. Opening his lips, he extended his tongue, thrusting it deeply within her as she settled herself, a gasp of pleasure echoing across the room.

Grinding herself onto his cock, Ava leaned forward and pulled Meghan to her, sharing a kiss as hot as the summer sun. Rocking slowly, she guided Meghan in a rhythm guaranteed to please them all.

Kissing and caressing each other, both ladies worked themselves into a frenzy using Jim's body. Grinding down on his tongue and cock, they rocked and moaned, kissed and enjoyed. Carefully, Ava fingered Meghan's clit, encouraging her to return the favor.

Her body already aflame with lust, Meghan quickly built to an orgasm as Ava's finger worked its magic and Jim's expert tongue thrust within her, his teeth occasionally nibbling the tender lips.

Trembling, she collapsed against Ava, her fingers still rubbing her lover's flesh. Grinding down hard on Jim's cock, Ava picked up her pace, driving them both quickly into an orgasm, their flesh slick with sweat and passion.

Her body trembling with fatigue, Meghan moved to lie against Jim, Ava soon settling on her other side. Curling to face Jim, she leisurely kissed him, allowing his tongue to share her sweet juices.

The rest of the evening and most of the next day, Meghan spent with Jim and Ava learning about Sapphic delights and enjoying Jim's watching. Occasionally, he would touch, lick and kiss, but never did his cock come near her pussy lips.

As she drove home late the next day, Meghan planned things for the following weekend, when Jim and Ava would be coming over to her house. Her pussy was already damp in anticipation, tingling for the hard length of Jim's cock.

As she pulled into her garage, she pressed the button for the door to close and flipped her skirt up. Pulling her panties aside, she fingered her clit as she imagined the feel of Jim's cock deep in her core. The weekend wouldn't be there quick enough.

MORE THAN HE BARGAINED FOR

A knock sounded on the door. She pulled the belt tighter on her robe and answered the door. Standing there, in the doorway was the appraiser her friend Tracy told her about. He smiled at her, and she shyly smiled back. Her eyes ran over him in a subtle way as she stepped back, allowing him to enter the foyer.

Jim couldn't believe the sight before his eyes. The tall redhead who answered the door was a knockout. Her 5 foot 8 inch frame, long bright red hair, and sparkling green eyes. She was wearing a green silk robe and he found himself wondering what she had on underneath it.

Julie smiled at the tall man. He had to be somewhere in his early thirties. She knew she was attractive and she knew she wanted him. Badly. From the bulge in the crotch of his dress slacks, she knew he found her attractive.

Having gotten over a messy divorce just months before, Jim was leery about dating again, but he did still have a sex drive like any normal man. He wandered about the living room, getting measurements and jotting notes down on his clipboard.

Julie's eyes followed his movements. The way his body looked in dress slacks, the pull of his button up shirt across his shoulders. The tie, that just begged to be removed. Mmm, this man was fine.

Jim moved on to the kitchen, conscious of Julie following him. She leaned against the counter and watched him. He cleared his throat softly.

"Um, Julie, I was wondering, may I have a glass of water?" he asked, his throat oddly dry.

"Yes silly." She replied and she stepped in front of him and reached around him to get a glass from the cabinet behind his head. For a moment Jim though of moving, but the view was just too nice. Her robe had parted slightly, allowing him to see her breasts. Part of his question was answered, she was not wearing a shirt or bra. Her chest pressed against his, her nipples hard, as she tried to reach the glasses. Their eyes met, and then their lips. Her hand left the glass on the shelf, and moved tot he back of his head. Drawn by the shear force of desire, the two kissed. Their tongues touched, then Julie became the aggressor, sure that if she didn't, he would pull back, apologize and leave.

Jim took the hint when her hand pressed against the bulge of his dress slacks, and caressed his cock through the soft material. The sound of a throat clearing had him glancing quickly to the doorway. A short blonde stood in the doorway. Like Julie she wore a robe, but hers was not belted and she definitely was not wearing anything under it. And for the view Jim got, he was sure beyond a doubt that she was a natural blonde.

One eyebrow arched. "Not interrupting anything am I'" she asked, though it was obvious to her that she was. Julie's hand continued to caress Jim's cock, he grew harder still at the stimulation and the view of two partially dressed ladies.

"Jim, I'd like you to met my lover, Stacy. We share everything. I hope you don't mind." Julie practically purred as she replied. Then she used her other hand to pull his shirt from inside his pants. Once it was free, she ran a hand up his chest.

Jim though that he had to be dreaming. Here was a mid thirties redhead woman, and her late twenties lover practically asking him to have sex with them.

"Would you like to see the bedroom now?" Julie asked as she stepped away from Jim. Stacy's eyes immediately fell to the bulge of Jim's pants.

"Uh yeah." He replied, not quite sure what was going on. He followed Julie and Stacy to their bedroom. Julie flipped on the lights, stepped into the room, then stripped off her robe. She wasn't wearing anything under her robe.

Stacy entered the room and did the same thing. Jim followed them, not quite sure what the rules of their game were, but for now, he wanted to play.

"Julie, you didn't tell him?" Stacy asked, before her lover could reply she turned to Jim and explained, "There is a standing rule in this house. If you enter the bedroom you have to strip, and before you can leave you have to orgasm. I though Julie had already told you from the way things looked earlier in the kitchen."

"Uh, no she didn't," Jim replied, unsure if they were joking or not. When both ladies approached him and began removing his clothes, he knew it was true. Their tender touch quickly aroused him as Julie removed his pants and Stacy his tie and shirt. She stopped to kiss his chest, then knelt down to remove his briefs as Julie stood up and kissed him. Her arms wrapped around him, and her body trapped Stacy between the two of them. Jim felt a light touch on his cock that he though was a fingertip, until his cock was swallowed in one try. Warm lips closed over the base of his head, and her groaned as Stacy moved back and forth, working his cock in her mouth. Julie moved back to the bed, and Stacy removed her mouth and stood. She grabbed Jim's hand and led him to the bed.

Julie watched her lover lead the man over to her. In his early thirty he was still in good shape. Obviously he cared for his body well, it definitely showed. Jim's cock stood hard and ready and she needed to feel that cock inside her so bad. Her fingers rubbed her nipple and clit as Stacy rolled condom onto Jim's cock. Then Jim climbed onto the bed. Julie rolled over so that her small tight ass faced Jim. Stacy moved onto the bed then up to the head of the bed so that she laid half under Julie's face, while facing Jim.

"I want her to eat me while you thrust into her." Jim slid his cock slowly into Julie, wanting the moment to last, knowing that when he started up a rhythm it would soon be over. It had been so long, too damn long.

Stacy watched his face as he sank deep into her lover. She knew it felt good for Julie, her tongue drove deep into Stacy's wet pussy and then darted out to tease her clit. Stacy slid one hand down her stomach to her clit and let Julie just tongue her pussy.

Jim slowly began to thrust into Julie's hot and tight pussy. It felt so good. So tight and wet. He slowly sped up, each time a little faster and a little harder of a thrust. Julie moaned into Stacy's pussy. Stacy lifted her hips up to Julie's face as she watched Jim. All three of them needed to cum. All three of them felt a tightened in their groins. Over and over Jim thrust into Julie's tight body. Stacy loved how her thrusts made Julie's tongue go in deeper. Oh yes, so deep. Julie came first, her tongue thrusting deep into Stacy. Jim thrust again and again, into Julie's pussy which had been flooded when she orgasmed, allowing his to go harder without worrying about hurting her. He rotated his hips slightly as he thrust, rubbing her clit with his finger, hoping to make her cum again. Stacy rocked faster and faster, her finger bringing herself to pleasure as Julie tongue thrust in and out of her pussy. Stacy came, releasing a light flood of juice into Julie's waiting mouth. Jim gave one last thrust and came, Julie's muscles clenching about him as she came again. He collapsed, half on, half off of Julie's soft and warm body. Soon all three shifted to be more comfortable.

Stacy lay to one side of Julie, Jim to the other. They both caressed the redhead's ample breasts. All three of them lay there thinking. Jim about how it had been so long, and how he had needed so badly to find an attractive willing women. About how fortunate he was to find two lovely women, who wanted him. Maybe being in his thirties and divorced wouldn't be so bad.

Stacy and Julie were both thinking the same thing, and smiling to themselves. It had been so long since they had had a threesome. Far too long, but that is what made it so good. After a while, they helped Jim get dressed and stayed out of the way while he finished his survey. The house was in great condition and would sell well. Both ladies were well pleased with his work that day.

REVELATIONS

Jared sighed, exhausted, running a callused hand through his wavy blonde hair, unable to focus on the legal brief before him.

"Quitting time," he thought, closing the folder as he reached for the intercom button on his phone.

"Patrick, I'm calling it quits for today."

"OK, buddy, drive carefully," a deep voice replied. "And say hello to your beautiful wife for me."

"Will do."

Jared smiled as he replaced the folder and locked the file cabinet, shrugging into his black leather bomber. Jessie, the night janitor, waved to him as he headed out of the office, the glass doors opening at a slight touch. He was out into the cool night air, the doors locking behind him.

Jared took a deep breath, enjoying the autumn breeze. He loved his car's cool leather seat, the purr of the engine as he shifted into drive. He drove home to the gentle sound of classical music, very little traffic on the road this long after rush hour.

With a sigh he turned off the ignition in the driveway, happy to be home. The muted sounds of a running shower met him inside the unlocked front door. With a smile he pictured his wife's petite form, her hands running soap over her body, likely stopping to tease her nipples and clit.

Jared restrained himself from joining her, his spirit more than willing but his body simply too tired. He headed to the kitchen instead, pouring a glass of water, and at the sink his eyes were drawn to the two glasses, both stained with lipstick.

"Good," he thought. "Cyndee needs to see more of her friends."

He was just settling into his favorite living-room chair when Cyndee came down the stairs, her black silk robe a perfect match for her long, glorious black hair. Quietly she moved behind him, her slender hands settling on his shoulders.

"Hello, love. How was work?"

Just her touch and her voice soothed Jared. Some days he wanted to cuddle against her and never move.

"Long. I'll never understand why I went into law. I should have opened a plant nursery."

Cyndee smiled and chuckled softly, music to Jared's ears.

"Because while the work may be hard and the laws often hard to understand, you, my love, thrive on the idealistic principles of truth, justice and the American way."

"Idealistic, huh?"

Jared grabbed her hands and guided Cyndee around to his lap. She snuggled against him, sighed, and then replied.

"Yes, you tend to see things as they should be, not as they truly are."

Jared thought he heard something else in her words, but shrugged it off as fatigue. His yawn confirmed it.

"I'd best take a shower and get to bed. I have to be at the office early."

Cyndee sighed and moved off his lap.

"Another long day?"

"Unfortunately."

* * *

Jared found himself remembering Cyndee's words the next day, and thinking of the two glasses in the sink.

She had mentioned an attraction to other women once, years ago when they were first dating, but never since. Now he felt a suspicion that troubled him. He loved Cyndee deeply, and it hurt that he could think this about her. He had to be wrong.

Jared placed a few quick calls. Pleading sudden illness, he left work shortly after two, four hours early.

The entire way home he cursed himself for even entertaining such thoughts, and he almost wrecked as he pulled into the driveway, another car already parked on his side.

Already he was imagining the scene he'd find: his wife talking with another woman, laughing at jokes, maybe just talking about nonsense. But when Jared opened the door he was greeted by the steady thump of rock music. Hesitantly he followed the music to its source, stopping just outside his bedroom door.

Slowly he turned the knob, then gently pushed the door open. His breath abandoned him and he felt faint when his eyes locked on his sweet wife, being thrust into by a dildo strapped to the body of a tall, slender blonde woman.

His beloved's hands were fisted in the sheets, her head thrashing on the bed. The sight aroused him as much as it angered him.

The song ended, and the pause before the next began was long enough for his wife's moans and a few of her words to reach his ears.

"Mmm, oh yes, Sabrina, yes. I need it harder, oh yes!"

Jared watched as the blonde thrust her hips again and again. Another song began, drowning out their moans, but not blinding him to their motion.

Sabrina's back began to arch, her body shaking. Cyndee's eyes closed and her body grew taut. The motion of both women stopped as they orgasmed as one and lay joined by a fake cock.

Sabrina rolled over and saw Jared first. She suddenly sat up, covering herself. Cyndee saw him, too, and leapt from the bed to turn off the stereo. She looked at him, her eyes pleading for understanding, Jared's own eyes glistening with tears that refused to fall.

"Jared ... please, I can explain."

Jared stood motionless, still not wanting to believe what was happening.

"Can you? It must be one hell of an explanation. I think you two should get dressed. I'll meet you downstairs when you're done."

Needing time to calm himself and figure just which emotion was strongest -- hurt, anger, or desire -- Jared headed toward the living room, the sounds of two women talking and frantically getting dressed following him down the hall.

He considered his options and his ten years of happiness with Cyndee. Did he really want to end it? Could they stay together? Could he survive without her? Was this his fault? Had he driven her to this? Would he always see her and Sabrina in his mind when he looked at his bed? Would the thought always arouse him?

Though an idealist, Jared also knew himself to be a little uptight, a man who didn't like change. Law had taught him to think logically, but his head was handing this issue to his heart, and that made this even harder.

"Jared?"

Her whisper pulled him out of his thoughts. Cyndee stood before him in jeans and a T-shirt, the afterglow of orgasm still clinging to her.

"Cyndee, sit down, please. You too, Sabrina."

They sat at opposite ends of the couch, stunned in wonder that he knew Sabrina's name. Jared resisted a sudden urge to laugh.

"Jared, I wanted to tell you last night. I even tried, but you were so tired. You have been too tired to make love to me for months now."

Jared nodded, hearing the truth in her words. Once he had made partner in his law office, his career had overwhelmed his life.

Knowing in his heart he'd forgive her, Jared tried to lighten the mood. Once he found forgiveness, he didn't have it in him to dwell on things.

"Well, I guess it could have been worse," he said. "You could have chosen a male lover instead of a woman who is in touch with her, er, masculine side."

Sabrina's head jerked up, her eyes meeting his. She knew what Jared was saying and what he meant by it, but Cyndee wasn't as quick.

"Jared, I never would have been with another man."

"Cyndee, let it go, OK?" smiling at her stunned expression. "It was a joke."

She didn't quite know what to think of his humor. She had expected him to be angry, not cracking jokes.

"Whaaat?"

"Let it go. What's done is done, just please don't hide this from me again. OK?"

"I ... you mean ... you forgive me?"

"I guess I have to, Cyndee. I love you. I could pretty much forgive you for anything. After all, I've forgiven you trying to food-poison me for the last ten years."

Sabrina chuckled, having first-hand knowledge of Cyndee's inadequate skills in the kitchen.

"Just don't hide it from me again. Tell me the truth, no matter what it is, and how much you think it will hurt me."

The room fell silent for a few moments, neither Jared nor Cyndee knowing what more to say.

Sabrina grinned to herself, deciding to focus on other things. Such as the memory of the bulge in Jared's pants when she first saw him in the doorway. He had been aroused. Hurt, yes, but aroused.

"So, tell me, Jared," she spoke up. "Did you enjoy watching me make love to Cyn?"

"Sabrina ... please, stop," Cyndee said. "Don't upset him."

Jared smiled.

"Honestly? Yes, I did."

He decided to play along with Sabrina's game, to see how far she would take it and how far Cyndee would let her go before she really put her foot down.

Cyndee sat stunned, not quite sure just what was happening. She was on an emotional roller-coaster, with no end to the ride in sight. She knew Sabrina was brazen and outgoing, two of the things that attracted her to her friend in the first place, but to say this?

And for Jared to admit it? Uptight Jared?

Cyndee felt a hand run up her thigh. She glanced up in shock, her eyes meeting Jared's smile. Sabrina leaned down and kissed her. Cyndee responded, hesitantly, her eyes open at first, focused on Jared. He leaned back in his chair, getting comfortable, and she closed her eyes.

Sabrina's tongue slid past her lips and rubbed against Cyndee's. Slowly they began to caress one other, tracing the paths of earlier, reawakening desire in each other.

Cyndee's jeans and T-shirt hit the floor, soon followed by Sabrina's dress and lingerie.

For the second time that day, Jared's eyes focused on a naked woman who was not his wife. Then his gaze was drawn to his petite wife's slender beauty. Of Asian decent, she was like a china doll, small, petite and utterly beautiful. Sabrina agreed, if her look of desire was any indication. Her hands gently stroked Cyndee's breasts and stomach, her lips moving over her face.

Sabrina moved to kneel between Cyndee's slightly spread legs. In return, Cyndee reached to caress her friend's breasts, her eyes focused once again on Jared. He smiled encouragingly, beginning to massage his cock through his slacks.

Cyndee shifted her focus to Sabrina, watching the desire darken her brown eyes to black. Gently she rolled her lover's nipples between her fingertips, delighting in the little moans of pleasure that followed.

Jared fought to loosen his tie and finally won the battle, tossing it to the chair with his shirt. His gaze remained locked on the women, their positioning on the couch giving him a wonderful view, in profile.

131

Sabrina pushed Cyndee's hands away and moved them to her own breasts. As Cyndee began to tweak and play with her own sensitive nipples, Sabrina caressed her thighs and gently touched her pussy lips. These light little touches reawakened Cyndee's desires, and by the time Sabrina's tongue gently flicked her clit, she was ready to scream.

Jared unzipped his trousers, no longer able to sit as a spectator, his cock aching badly to be stroked. His pants and boxers went together and he settled back in the chair, palming his hardness. After months of going without, his cock suddenly let him know of its feeling of neglect. All ready he could feel the beginnings of orgasm. Groaning, he slowed down, trying to make it last.

Cyndee slid down on the couch, driving her aching pussy into Sabrina's face, her hands grasping the back of Sabrina's head, intertwined in her hair, her tongue right where she wanted it to be.

Cyndee's gasps filled the room as her lover's skilful tongue drove her over the edge.

Sabrina's head lifted, and she smiled at Jared. She stood, gracefully, Cyndee still prone, dazed on the couch, surprised that her wild Irish lass had stopped. Strutting, aware of her sensuality, Sabrina walked toward Jared. His hands continued to please his eager cock.

When she stood only inches from him, she turned and looked at Cyndee. Her head was resting on the back of the couch, but her eyes were open, eager to see the next move.

With no resistance coming from the wife, Sabrina turned back to the husband. His hand continued to leisurely stroke up and down the hard length of his cock. His blue eyes were slightly glazed, but still held her gaze.

Moving slowly, she climbed into his lap and leaned back against him, one of her legs on either side of his right thigh. His right arm wrapped around her and she shifted slightly, his cock free and easy to access as she began to caress her own pussy. Jared brushed his hand down the side of her breast, his eyes flashing between Cyndee and Sabrina's pussy.

Cyndee stood and approached them. Carefully she slid the footrest over to the left side of Jared and knelt on it, balancing herself half over his left leg as she began to caress his cock.

Jared stroked Cyndee's back with his left hand and Sabrina's right side and leg with his right. Cyndee's lips locked over his cock as Sabrina began thrusting against her fingertips. She moaned over and over as sensations built. Jared hadn't realized just how close he was to orgasm until Cyndee's tongue began to flick against his head each time she pulled back.

Her warm, wet mouth felt almost as good as the pussy he remembered. Sabrina's thrusts grew faster and harder, her ass grinding against Jared's thigh, her head rolling back against his shoulder as her back arched. Waves of orgasm tightened her pussy around her fingers. Her juices leaked onto his thigh, the aroma heightening Jared's arousal.

Cyndee's suction grew stronger, pulling Jared's cock deeper into her mouth. She could feel it pulsing, and finally he came. After several months, the strength of his orgasm overwhelmed him. It felt so good. Cyndee swallowed all of his cum, delighting in the salty sweetness. Regardless of how much she enjoyed Sabrina's sweet juices, Jared's salty cum would always be her favorite.

Sabrina pulled back and laid her head against his side as Jared drew gasping breaths, his mind still reeling from his orgasm. Sabrina shifted on his lap and Cyndee climbed off the footrest, grabbing the throw-blanket off the back of the couch and climbing onto the other half of Jared's lap. Carefully she and Sabrina covered the three of them up.

Jared smiled as they laid their heads against his chest. A sudden stitch in his side reminded him just how uncomfortable this position could be.

"Um, seeing as how I am not as young as I used to be, do you think we could take the cuddling to the bedroom?" he asked.

Giggling, Sabrina and Cyndee hopped off his lap and pretended to help the "old man" out of his chair and up the stairs. With hearty laughter, all three fell onto the bed, romping and tickling a bit before they settled back down to cuddle.

As the night passed, the two ladies did their best to coax the 'old man' into arousal again, and to their delight, succeeded. As dawn threaded its yellow rays through the sky, all three fell into an exhausted, fulfilled sleep.

THREE ON A KING SIZED BED

Shivering as a cool breeze drifted in through the open window, Chrys rolled over and cuddled against the warmth of her lover. Jason sighed in his sleep and pulled her closer. With a soft moan of contentment, she snuggled closer and ready to go back to sleep.

She had just closed her eyes when the bed dipped. A nip at the base of her neck slightly startled her. Chrys signed softly as Erin slid a hand over her hip and spooned against her back.

"Miss me lover?"

"Mmmm." Chrys managed to murmur, her mind still wrapped in slumber.

Jason's eyes fluttered open and a tender smile crossed his lips as he responded, "Hi Erin. I missed you."

"I'm sure you did." Erin leaned over Chrys' body, her bare breasts pressing against the blonde's back. "And I missed you too baby." Her lips pressed against his, their tongues dueling while Chrys watched, her pussy tingling.

Feeling left out, she nudged her way in, snaking her tongue out for an erotic three-way kiss, just the way she liked it. Jason pulled back first, his hands busily roaming over both sets of feminine bodies as the women twisted positions, curling into each other, legs intertwined.

Chrys positioned herself straddled beneath her naked lover. Erin's hands quickly went to work, peeling away her silk nightgown, baring her breasts to the cool night air.

"Erin!" Chrys gasped. "It's cold."

She could feel her nipples beading at the sudden temperate change. Erin just grinned, and leaned down, nuzzling her face in the gently sloped valley.

Not to be left out, Jason moved down the bed to Chrys' ankles and worked his way back up, pressing kisses against her legs, pausing to nibble here and there as she squirmed under him.

"I missed you," she gasped as Erin tongued one of her nipple and gently bit down.

Erin responded by moving up further, and pressing her lips to Chrys' neck. "And I missed you too," she whispered, her heated breath mingling with Chrys' moments before her tongue took possession of her lover's mouth.

Chrys moaned and shifted beneath the brunette's lithe form as Jason's questing lips pressed against her inner thigh. Opening her legs wider while thrusting her tongue into Erin's mouth, she granted him further access. His calloused hands slid up her hips to where Erin's thighs spread over her, and up her lover's body, pulling her down to his level.

Mound to mound, they laid pressed together, exchanging wet, carnal kisses as Jason's tongue alternated between their two dripping pussies. She couldn't help but feel light headed at the tender love and devotion her lovers were sharing with her. Ever since she had proposed the idea of them all moving in together over a year before, she hadn't once regretted it. Jealousy hadn't come up, and Jason and Erin had taken to each other right from the first.

Reaching her sexual height, Chrys twisted her head to the side and looked down the subtle curves of her lover's body to the toned blond settled between her legs. "More," she demanded as their gazes met.

Flashing her a grin, Jason moved to the side. Erin soon followed, sliding slowly down her body, her pussy leaving a wet trail along Chrys' right leg. She shifted to the side and settled on her knees next to Chrys.

"Grab a condom, lover," Erin asked.

Chrys sat up while Jason leaned over to the nightstand and grabbed a foil packet. As soon as he had settled himself between them again, Erin snagged the packet from his hand and tore it open with her teeth. Chrys placed a hand under his balls, cupping the smooth sac in her palm while Erin placed the tip of the latex between her lips, leaned down, and rolled the condom on slowly with her teeth.

Watching her girlfriend slowly encase their lover in latex, she couldn't help but shiver. It was so damn erotic watching Erin's pouty red lips wrapping around Jason's cock.

As she reached the base, Jason jerked, his balls tightening in Chrys' hand. Gently, he tangled his fingers in Erin's shoulder length hair, caressing her as she shifted back, and then sucked his length back into the warm velvet of her mouth.

Chrys moved around behind Erin, running her hands over the brunette's smooth skin, until she reached Erin's parted thighs. Dipping a finger past the moist lips of her lover's sex, then thrust deep, earning a whimpered moan in respond.

"Feel good baby?"

"Mmmm," Erin responded, her mouth full of cock.

Adding another finger, Chrys worked them in and out of her lover's tight channel, getting her creamy wet and ready for Jason's cock.

"You want more than this?"

Erin pulled back, Jason's cock slipping from her mouth with a faint pop. "Yes."

Chrys pulled her fingers free, and dropped the cream coated digits to her own lap. "Then lay back." As Erin rolled onto her back, Chrys teased her own clit. Jason quickly moved between the brunette's thighs and positioned his cock-head against her flushed and swollen nether lips.

"Yes," Erin said, as she arched against him. "Fuck me, hard and good, while I lick some sweet pussy."

Chrys watched for a moment as her lovers shifted into position, and settled into a slow rhythm, before swinging a leg over Erin's head and lowering her pussy to her mouth.

Wasting no time, Erin licked and nibbled at the outer folds, before thrusting her tongue deeply into Chrys' pussy, as Jason's thrusts arched her up and into Chrys moist flesh.

"Damn Erin, you're so tight baby." His voice dropped a pitch. Already husky, his words fairly dripped with molasses and old world charm.

Erin murmured against Chrys' pussy, her words lost but the meaning clear, especially when she pumped her hips faster into Jason's thrusts.

Jason gripped her hips, timing his thrusts against her, even as he picked up speed."Come for me baby, cream all over my cock so Chrys can lick it clean."

Chrys moved her hips to Jason's increased rhythm, rocking her hips in time to his thrusts while Erin feasted on her nectar, until she could lean down and engage Jason in a kiss. Her fingers found and played with Erin's nipples, tweaking and pinching the tender buds.

Tongues dueling for dominance, they worked together, grinding against Erin. The three of them formed an erotic triangle as the nimble brunette worked her tongue in and out of Chrys core to their combined tempo.

Thrust and withdrawal, grind and lift, until Erin arched her back, and sank down into Jason's thrusts. Removing a hand from her lover's breasts, Chrys manipulated her own clit, twirling a fingertip over the tiny, swollen bud, eliciting a wave of response through her body.

Her pussy tingling, Chrys shifted off of Erin as she thrashed on the bed, a sign she was about to come. And sure enough, she did, with a soft scream echoing through the room. Jason continued to ride her through her orgasm, until her gasps turned to soft, fulfilled moans.

Chrys smiled as her lover's eyes opened, a soft dreamy light filling them.

Sweat beading on his forehead, Jason moved back, kneeling between the brunette's sprawled legs. "You're turn baby," he drawled.

Still pinching her clit, playing with the tender bud, Chrys moved to kneel beside Erin, careful not to put to much weight on her left leg as she leaned down and took Jason's cock in her mouth. Although she couldn't taste him through the latex, she could taste Erin. Her musky, sweet cream, coating the thin barrier. "Oh God Chrys, that's feel so good." Tightening her lips, Chrys worked her mouth slowly up and down Jason's cock, teasing him until he had finally had enough and gripping her hand gently in his hands, he guided her away.

His hands slid down to her shoulders and firmly Jason pushed Chrys to her back and moved to cover her, nudging her legs apart. Wrapping her legs around his waist, she settled him in the soft vee of her body. As soon as his cock-head pressed against her lips, Chrys arched against him, working his cock slowly into her needy core.

"Damn baby," he drawled, his good 'ol boy accent showing through. "You feel so good wrapped around my cock like that."

She gasped and clenched her pussy tightly around him, milking his cock as he worked it slowly all the way in, then out so that just an inch teased her drenched flesh.

"Would you...stop teasing and finish what you two started?"

In response, Jason slammed against her, thrusting so hard and deep she saw stars for a moment. "Yes. That's what I'm talking about."

The bed creaked beneath them as he pounded away at her, fucking her harder than he had their petite lover. She relished the physical pounding that her mostly lesbian lover abstained from. And it never failed to amaze Chrys the way Jason shifted between the two, playing tender almost submissive lover to Erin and alpha dominant to her. If anything, it made her love him more.

"More, harder, faster," she chanted in time to his wild thrusts. Beside them, Erin watched, her green eyes heavy lidded.

Blue gaze locked with his, Chrys maintained eye contact even as she felt the faint stirrings of ecstasy deep within her core. Every nerve awake and inflamed, she arched her sweat glistening body against his, begging for his rough fucking.

"More," she demanded, her breath coming out in harsh gasps. She could feel the roughness of his hands gripping her hips, pulling her harder against him with each thrust, until her body throbbed with each heart beat and she soared. Tightening her legs around his waist, she locked him in place against her body as her pussy quivered around his cock, milking him into mutual climax.

Unceremoniously, he collapsed on top of her, his sweaty body against hers as she coasted along, still aware of the sensations flooding her body.

"Baby, you're too good to me," he panted, every word followed by a quick breath. Rolling to the side, he lay motionless until he caught his breath again.

The desire to sleep coursed through her body and Chrys snuggled against Erin and cooed softly as the brunette stroked the back of her head, soothing her from pleasure to the gently lethargic state that follows it.

Jason pressed soft kisses against her spine, his hands brushing slowly over them both.

Regret evident in his voice, Jason said, "As much as I'd love to stay here and cuddle with you two, I've got to get to work." The bed dipped as he sat up. Chrys had to smile softly at the tender, yearning gleam in his eyes.

"Although, I do have some sick time."

Laughing softly Chrys batted his hands away as he moved to palm her breasts. "Go to work you."

His eyes resembling a puppy, Jason mournfully gazed at her breasts then huffed a sigh. "If I have to."

Chrys patiently waited as he kissed Erin goodbye.

As he leaned in to press a leisurely kiss against Chrys lips, she reached down and cupped his sweaty balls in her hand. Slipping her tongue into his mouth, she rubbed his cock sensuously before pulling away. "Make sure you get off on time tonight. We'll be here waiting."

Heat flaring in his eyes, Jason climbed off the bed and moved across the room to the bathroom door.

"Better get my ass to work then so I can get started." With a playful wink, he stepped into the bathroom and closed the door.

"You're a tease you know," Erin mumbled.

"I know. But after spending all day thinking up ways he's going to fuck us senseless, he's going to be wild tonight. You should know that by now."

" I remember the last time you teased him like that. You would up tied to the head board while we licked ice cream and cake off of your body."

As the sound of the shower drifted through the door, Chrys settled against Erin, cuddling into her lover's arms.

"Oh, I definitely remember. That why I made sure to stock up on cherries and strawberries when I went to the grocery store earlier."

Erin's soft snore was her only response.

Michelle Houston

* * *

ABOUT THE AUTHOR

Born to ride on the back of dragons, to journey among the stars in a ship traveling faster than light, or to dance the night away in the arms of a mysterious vampire, Michelle Houston willingly shares the worlds in her mind in an effort to bring them to life.

Writing everything from short and sweet stories, to hot and spicy tales of kink, from contemporary tales of erotic romance to erotica romances featuring Greek gods, vampires and were-creatures, she has crossed sexualities and has gone wherever her mental muse has guided her, a journey she has never regretted.

As for the more mundane details: Michelle is a Sagittarius, born in the Chinese zodiac Year of the Horse. She currently resides in the Midwest US with her husband and daughter. Michelle has a love of the natural world around us (except for insects, spiders, snakes, scorpions, and she reserves the right to add more at any time). She's one of those people that actually liked Biology in High School, and enjoys learning about all things science.

In other words, she is an ordinary woman with an imagination that is only held in bounds by how fast she can type.

You can find out more about Michelle Houston on her author website at: www.michellehouston.com

www.ingramcontent.com/pod-product-compliance
Lightning Source LLC
Chambersburg PA
CBHW060617130626
46555CB00002B/544